The Book of
Elves and Fairies

Frances Jenkins Olcott

DOVER PUBLICATIONS, INC.
Mineola, New York

Published in the United Kingdom by David & Charles, Brunel House, Forde Close, Newton Abbot, Devon TQ12 4PU.

Bibliographical Note

This Dover edition, first published in 2002, is an original selection of stories from the edition published by Houghton Mifflin Company, Boston and New York, in 1918.

Library of Congress Cataloging-in-Publication Data

Olcott, Frances Jenkins.
    The book of elves and fairies / Frances Jenkins Olcott.
       p. cm.
    Selections from the book of the same name, originally published: Boston : Houghton Mifflin Co., 1918.
    Summary: An anthology of stories and poems from around the world about the residents of Fairyland.
    ISBN 0-486-42364-6 (pbk.)
    1. Fairy tales. 2. Tales. 3. Children's poetry. [1. Fairy tales. 2. Folklore. 3. Poetry—Collections.] I. Title.

PZ5.O43 Bo 2002
398.2—dc21
[[Fic]]   2002067687

Manufactured in the United States of America
Dover Publications, Inc., 31 East 2nd Street, Mineola, N.Y. 11501

Contents

To
Theodore Olcott Phillips

"Good luck befriend thee, son; for, at thy birth,
The FAIRY LADIES danced upon the hearth;
The drowsy nurse hath sworn she did them spy
Come tripping to the room, where thou didst lie,
And sweetly singing round about thy bed
Strew all their blessings on thy sleeping head!"
—MILTON

The Book of
Elves and Fairies

I. The Fairies' Story Hour

COME! COME!
TO THE FAIRIES' STORY HOUR!

IN THE MOONLIT MEADOW

Fairies! Fairies everywhere! Hear them come! See them come in the pale moonlight to this lovely meadow! They rush through the air; they throng from the wood; they spring up from the ground; they peep from the flowers and leaves. They are all hastening to the Fairies' Story Hour. The Midsummer moon is shining, shining; while the Midsummer breeze is swaying, swaying the harebells, lilies, and grasses.

Laughter! whisper! Laughter! whisper! See, through the air comes gliding a whole host of radiant little Fairies. They poise lightly on their silvery wings, and float down to the harebells and lilies. They flicker over the meadow like gay butterflies. Laughter! whisper!

Hum! whirr! Hum! whirr! What is that noise in the tree-tops? From among the dark leaves fly hundreds and hundreds of broad-backed beetles, bumping and thumping each other. They are followed by a silent cloud of bats, that wheel and whirl, and flap their leathery wings. And to the back of every beetle and every bat clings a tiny roguish Elf peeping down at the meadow below.

Rap! tack! tack! Rap! tack! tack! From behind each tree-trunk steps a little Leprechaun as big as your thumb. They are the Fairy Shoemakers. Their long beards and red caps wag in the moonlight; and the little men smile and chuckle to themselves, for well they know where the pots of Fairy Gold are hidden. Near them, peering from behind stones and bushes, are the Curmudgeons, rolling their mischievous eyes.

1

Skip! skip! Knock! knock! What have we here? From out of the earth pours a swarm of little Spriggans and Pixies gaily dressed, and Knockers with their tiny hammers in their tiny hands. They have left the meadows and moors; they have left the mines of tin and copper, and the diamond caves, to come to the Fairies' Story Hour. How they hustle, how they bustle, out of the earth!

Gallop-a-trot! Gallop-a-trot! What comes from the wood? A long line of prancing goats and house-cats! And on the back of each is a House-Elf, to be sure! The Brownies, the Boggarts, the Tomts, the Piskeys, are all there. They have left their snug corners in human homes; they have left cellars, barns, and threshing-floors; they have left bowls of clubbered cream on warm hearthstones, to come to the Fairies' Story Hour. And who is this that lights their way with a Will-o'-the-Wisp lantern? 'Tis Robin Goodfellow, freakish Elf! Ho! Ho! Ho!

Sing! cling! Sing! cling! What are these that come sailing through the air? Mother-of-pearl boats with coral masts and sails of sea-lace! Each little boat is crowded with Sea-Queens and Water-Fairies. Their green hair is long and flowing, and their robes are of rainbow spray. And near them, astride frisky sea-horses, are the Kelpies, blowing loudly on their conch-shell trumpets. And each Kelpie is armed with a shield of pearl and a sword-fish weapon. They have all left the foaming green waves and the pink coral palaces to come to the Fairies' Story Hour.

Now! Listen! Listen! The harebells and lilies are ringing sweet music, while from meadow flowers and acorn-cups and forest nuts tumble lazy, sleepy Elves rubbing their eyes, and hastening to join the others at the Fairies' Story Hour.

The harebells and lilies ring louder and louder. And from out the cool wood step King Oberon and Queen Mab, with all their Fairy train that glitters in the moonshine like a long string of jewels.

The royal train advances into the middle of the meadow. The King and Queen seat themselves on a throne of moss. At their left is capering Puck mowing and mouthing; at their right, Ariel the sweetest singer. All present bow themselves before the throne.

See! Queen Mab raises her wand, and each little Elf and Fairy scurries and hurries to make himself comfortable. Some sway on the blades of grass; others climb the flower stalks and curl up inside the fragrant blossoms; while still others swing and rock in the trees, or nestle among the ferns and under toadstool umbrellas.

Every wee Elf, and every tiny Fairy, and every little Imp, from all the world over, is here. Indeed, all the members of the entire Fairy Family are present except the human-sized ones. They are too busy to come. The Elfin Princes are searching cottages and palaces for mortal brides to carry off to Fairyland. The Elfin nurses are leaving Changelings in babies' cradles; while the Fairy Godmothers are far away bestowing wonderful gifts on good children, and punishing bad ones.

Look! Look! Queen Mab waves her wand! The Fairies' Story Hour is beginning. All is hushed.

Listen now to the Fairy tales.

II. Around! Around! In Fairy Rings!

ADVENTURES OF
ROBIN GOODFELLOW

From Merry England

HOW ROBIN GOODFELLOW WAS BORN

Once upon a time, when men did eat more and drink less, when men did know no knavery, there were wont to walk many harmless sprites called Fairies, dancing in brave order in Fairy Rings on green hills, to sweet music. These sprites would make themselves invisible, and many mad pranks would they play, pinching careless housemaids black and blue, and turning ill-kept houses topsy-turvy. But lovingly they would use neat housemaids, giving them silver and other pretty toys with which they left in the maids' shoes and pockets, or in bright kitchen pans.

Now, in those Fairy days there was born on earth a tiny Elfin boy whom folk called Robin Goodfellow. And wonderful were the gifts from Fairyland that came to Robin when he was a baby. In his room suddenly would appear rich embroidered cushions, delicate linen garments, and all sorts of delicious things to eat and drink. So he was never in want.

Now, when Robin was grown to six years, he was so mischievous that the neighbours all complained of his pranks until he was forced to run away.

He wandered about until he began to get hungry; then, going to a tailor, he took service with him. He remained there until he grew so mischievous that he was obliged to run away again.

HOW HE RECEIVED A MESSAGE
FROM FAIRYLAND

After he had travelled a good day's journey from the tailor's house, he sat down by the wayside and, being weary, fell asleep. No sooner had he closed his eyes than he fancied he saw tiny beings tripping on the grass before him, to the sound of sweet music. And when he awoke, he found, to his surprise, a scroll lying near by on which were these verses, written in letters of gold:—

> *"Robin, my only son and heir,*
> *For food and drink take thou no care.*
> *Wish what thou wilt, and thou shalt have*
> *The power to tease both fool and knave.*
> *Change when thou wilt thine Elfish shape,*
> *To horse, or hog, or dog, or ape;*
> *And scare each idle dirty maid,*
> *And make all wicked men afraid.*
> *But love thou those that honest be,*
> *And help them in necessity.*
>
> *"Do thus, and all the world shall know*
> *The pranks of Robin Goodfellow.*
> *If thou'lt observe my just command,*
> *One day thou shalt see Fairyland."*

Robin, having read this, was very joyful, for he perceived that he had Fairy power. He straightway wished for something to eat, and it appeared before him. Then he wished himself a horse, and no sooner did he say so than he became a handsome colt, curveting and leaping about. He wished himself a dog, and was one. After that he turned himself into any shape he liked. Then taking his own form again, he once more started on his travels.

OF HIS MAD PRANKS—HO! HO! HO!

And from that time forward many were the merry tricks Robin played on those he met.

Once, seeing a rude and clownish fellow searching for a lost horse, Robin turned himself into a horse, and led the rude man a chase over field and briar, until he allowed the man to catch him and mount his back. Then Robin jumped into a stream and, turning into a fish, swam to the shore and ran away, laughing, "Ho! Ho! Ho!"—leaving the man to get out of the water as best he could.

At night Robin often visited farmers' houses, and helped the neat housemaids with their work, breaking their hemp, dressing their flax, and spinning their yarn. One night he came to a house where there was a good and handsome maid. And while she slept Robin did her work, more than she could have done in twelve hours. The maid wondered the next morning to see all done so finely, and that night she watched to see what would follow.

At twelve of the clock in came Robin and, singing, fell to work breaking her hemp and doing her spinning, and as he worked he sang a mad song:—

> *"Within and out, in and out, round as a ball,*
> *With hither and thither, as straight as a line,*
> *With lily and germander, and sops of wine,*
> *With sweetbriar,*
> *And bonfire,*
> *And strawberry wire,*
> *And columbine!"*

The maid, seeing that he had no clothes, pitied him, and the next night she laid out a little suit that she had cut and sewed during the day. Robin, coming in, spied the clothes, whereat he started, and said:—

> *"'Tis not your garments new or old*
> *That Robin loves. I feel no cold.*
> *Had you left me milk or cream,*
> *You should have had a pleasant dream,*
> *Because you left no drop or crumb,*
> *Robin never more will come."*

And with that he ran out of the door, laughing loudly, "Ho! Ho! Ho!"

And many other mad pranks did Robin Goodfellow play. At times he turned himself into a will-o'-the-wisp, misleading lovers who came over the heath; at other times he punished knaves and idle maids, or rewarded good and worthy people. And always he ran laughing, "Ho! Ho! Ho!"

HOW HE DANCED IN THE FAIRY RING

At length Oberon, King of Fairyland, seeing so many honest and merry tricks, called one night to Robin as he lay sleeping in the greenwood:—

> *"Robin, my son, come, quickly rise!*
> *First stretch, then yawn, and rub your eyes.*
> *For you must go with me to-night*
> *To dance with Fairy, Elf, and Sprite.*
> *Come quickly now, my roguish son,*
> *'Tis time our sports were well begun."*

Robin, hearing this, woke and rose hastily, and, looking about, saw in the moonlight King Oberon, and many Fairies with him dressed in green silk. And all these did welcome Robin Goodfellow into their company.

King Oberon took Robin by the hand and led him a dance. And near by sat little Tom Thumb, the Fairy piper, no bigger than a plum. His bagpipe was made of a wren's quill and the skin of a tiny bug. This pipe made music so shrill and sweet, that naught might be compared to it.

Then all the Fairies for joy did circle Robin around, and in a ring did dance about him; and Robin Goodfellow danced in the midst of them, and sang this song:—

> *"Quick and nimble!*
> *Quick and nimble!*
> *Round about little ones!*
> *In and out, wheel about,*
> *Run, hop, or amble!*

> *"Elves, Urchins, Goblins all, and little Fairies,*
> *Who do pinch black and blue, idle maids in dairies,*
> *Make a ring on the grass, with your quick measures.*
> *Tom shall play, and I will sing, for all your pleasures.*

"Quick and nimble!
Quick and nimble!
Round about little ones!
In and out, wheel about,
Run, hop, or amble!"

Thus they danced for a good space, then sat themselves down upon the grass, and the Fairies told Robin of many Elfish tricks and merry capers; until, the time passing, a shepherd in a field near by blew his pipes so loudly that he frightened little Tom Thumb.

The Fairies punished the shepherd by the loss of his pipes, so that they presently broke in his hand, to his great amazement. Hereat Robin Goodfellow laughed, "Ho! Ho! Ho!"

The morning being come, at cock-crow the Fairies hastened away to Fairyland, where I think they yet remain.

THE POTATO SUPPER

From Ireland

Some folk say that the Little People, the Fairies, were once angels that were cast out of Heaven for their sins. They fell to earth and grew smaller and smaller. And to-day they dance on moonlit nights in Fairy Rings, and play all manner of pranks.

Be that as it may, one night a merry troop of them was capering in the moonshine. On a nice green sward by a river's bank the little fellows were dancing hand-in-hand, with their red caps wagging at every bound. And so light were their feet that the dew trembled, but was not disturbed. So they danced, spinning around and around, and twirling, and bobbing, and diving, until one of them chirped:—

> *"Cease! Cease with your humming!*
> *Here's an end to your mumming!*
> *By my smell*
> *I can tell*
> *That a Priest is now coming!"*

And away all the Fairies scampered as fast as they could. Some hid under the green leaves of the Foxglove, their little caps peeping out like crimson bells. Others crept under the shadow of stones, or beneath the bank of the river.

And scarcely had they done so, when along came Father Horrigan riding slowly on his pony. He was thinking to himself that he would end his journey at the first cabin he came to. And so he did, for soon he stopped at the little house of Dermod Leary, and, lifting the latch, walked in with: "A blessing on all here!"

And a welcome guest, you may be sure, was Father Horrigan, for no man was better loved in all that country. But when Dermod saw him enter, he was troubled, for he had nothing to offer for supper except some potatoes that his wife was boiling in a pot over the fire. Then he remembered that he had set a net in the river. "There'll be no harm," thought he, "in my stepping down to see if anything has been caught."

So down to the river went Dermod. He found as fine a salmon in the net as ever jumped from water. But as he was taking it out, the net was jerked from his hands, and away the salmon went, swimming along as though nothing had happened.

Dermod looked sorrowfully at the wake that the fish left shining like a line of silver in the moonlight.

"May bitter luck attend you night and day!" cried he, shaking his fist. "Some evil thing sure it was that helped you, for did I not feel it pull the net out of my hand!"

"You're all wrong, Dermod! There were a hundred or more of us pulling against you!" squeaked a little voice near his feet, and the whole troop of Fairies—hundreds and hundreds of them—came rushing from their hiding-places, and stood before him, their red caps nodding violently.

Dermod gazed at them in wonder; then one of the Fairies said:—

"Make yourself noways uneasy about the Priest's supper, Dermod Leary. If you will go back and ask him one question for us, there'll be as fine a supper spread before him in no time, as ever was put on table."

"I'll have nothing to do with you at all, at all!" answered Dermod; "I know better than to sell my soul to the likes of you!"

But the little Fairy was not to be repulsed. "Will you ask the Priest just one civil question for us, Dermod?" said he.

Dermod considered for a moment. "I see no objection," said he, "to the same. But I'll have nothing to do with your supper, mind that!"

The Little People all crowded near him, while the Fairy answered:—

"Go and ask Father Horrigan to tell us whether our souls will be saved at the Last Day. And, if you wish us well, Dermod Leary, you will bring the word that he says."

Away went Dermod to his cabin.

"Please, your reverence," said he to Father Horrigan, "may I make bold to ask your honour a question?"

"What is it?" said Father Horrigan.

"Why, then," said Dermod, "will the souls of the Little People be saved at the Last Day?"

"Who bids you ask that question, Leary?" said Father Horrigan, fixing his eyes sternly on Dermod.

"I'll tell no lies about the matter, nothing in life but the truth," answered Dermod. "'Twas the Little People themselves who sent me. They are in thousands down on the bank of the river waiting for your word."

"Go back," said Father Horrigan, "and tell them that if they want to know they must come here to me themselves, and I'll answer that and any other question."

So back Dermod hurried to the river. The Fairies came swarming around him. They pressed close to his feet, with faces upturned as they anxiously waited. And Dermod, brave man that he was, spoke out boldly and gave them the Priest's message. And when they heard that, the whole multitude of little Fairies uttered shrill cries and groans; and they whisked past Dermod in such numbers that he was quite bewildered. Then in a trice he found himself alone.

He went slowly back to his cabin. He opened the door. The fire was burning brightly. The candles were lighted. And good Father Horrigan was seated comfortably at the table, a pitcher of new milk before him, and a bit of fresh butter, from Dermod's cow. And Dermod's wife was handing him a big, handsome potato, whose white, mealy insides were bursting through its skin, and smoking like a hard-ridden horse on a frosty night.

Dermod sat down at the table, and began to eat without a word. And when Father Horrigan was through the good Priest smacked his lips, and said that he had relished the hot tasty potatoes, more than a dozen fat salmon, and a whole Fairy feast!

THE MILK-WHITE CALF
AND THE FAIRY RING

From Ireland

In Tipperary is one of the most singularly shaped hills in the world. It has a peak at the top like a conical nightcap. On this very peak, long years ago, a herdsman spent his nights and days watching the herd. Now, the hill was ancient Fairy ground, and the Little People were angry that the scene of their light and airy gambols should be trampled by the rude hoofs of bulls and cows. The lowing of the cattle sounded sad in their ears. So the Queen of the Fairies determined to drive away the herdsman.

One night the moon shone brightly on the hill. The cattle were lying down. The herdsman, wrapped in his mantle, was watching the twinkling stars, when suddenly there appeared before him a great horse with the wings of an eagle, and the tail of a dragon. This beast hissed loudly and spat fire, and, while the herdsman was looking on, half dead with fright, it turned into a little old man, lame of leg, with a bull's head around which flames were playing.

The next moment the little old man changed into a huge ape, with duck's feet, and a turkey-cock's tail. And then the Queen of the Fairies—for of course it was she—roared, neighed, hissed, bellowed, howled, and hooted so fearfully that the poor herds-man in terror covered his head with his mantle. But it was of no use, for with one puff of wind she blew away the fold of his man-tle, let him hold it never so tightly. As for the poor man, he could not stir or close his eyes, but was forced to sit there gazing at this terrible sight until his hair lifted his hat half a foot from his head, and his teeth chattered so that they almost fell out of his mouth.

Meanwhile the frightened cattle scampered about like mad, as if bitten by fleas, and so they continued to do until the sun rose. Then the Fairy Queen disappeared.

12

Night after night, the same thing happened, and the cattle went mad. Some fell into pits, or tumbled into the river and were drowned. By and by, not a herdsman was willing to tend the cattle at night. The farmer who owned the hill offered triple and quadruple wages, but not a man was found who would face the terrors of the Fairy Ring. The herd gradually thinned, and the Fairies, on moonlit nights, danced and gambolled as merrily as before, sipping dewdrops from acorn-cups, and spreading their feasts on the heads of mushrooms.

Now, there dwelt in that part of the country a man named Larry Hoolahan, who played on the pipes better than any other player within fifteen parishes. A dashing, roving blade was Larry, and afraid of nothing. One day the farmer met him, and told him all his misfortunes.

"If that is what ails you," said Larry, "make your mind easy. Were there as many Fairies on the hill as there are potato-blossoms in Tipperary, I would face them. It would be a queer thing, indeed, if I, who was never afraid of a proper man, should turn my back on a Fairy not the bigness of one's thumb!"

"Larry," said the farmer, "do not talk so bold, for you know not who is hearing you! But, if you make your words good, and watch my herds for a week on top of the hill, your hand shall be free of my dish till the sun has burnt itself down to the bigness of a farthing rushlight!"

The bargain was struck, and Larry went to the hill-top when the moon was beginning to peep over its brow. He took his seat on a big stone under a hollow of the hill, with his back to the wind, and pulled out his pipes.

He had not played long when the voices of the Fairies were heard upon the blast like a low stream of music. Presently they burst into a loud laugh, and Larry could plainly hear one say:—

"What! Another man upon the Fairies' Ring! Go to him, Queen, and make him repent of his rashness!"

And away they flew, and Larry felt them pass by his face like a swarm of midges. Looking up hastily he saw, between the moon and him, a great black cat, standing on the very tip of its claws, with its back up, and mewing with a voice like a water-mill.

Presently it swelled up toward the sky, and, turning round on its left hind leg, whirled till it fell to the ground. Then it started up in the shape of a salmon with a cravat round its neck, and wearing a pair of new top-boots.

"Go on, my jewel!" said Larry. "If you dance, I'll pipe," and he struck up.

But the Queen of the Fairies—for of course it was she—turned into this and that and the other; but still Larry played on, as well as he knew how. At last she lost patience, and changed herself into a calf, milk-white as the cream of Cork, and with eyes as mild as those of a loving girl.

She came up gentle and fawning, hoping to throw him off his guard, and then to work him some wrong. But Larry was not so deceived, for when she came near, dropping his pipes, he leaped on her back.

Now, from the top of the hill, as you look westward, you may see the broad river Shannon, full ten miles away. On this night its waters shone beautifully under the moon, and no sooner had Larry leaped on the back of the Fairy Queen than she sprang from the hill-top, and bounded clear at one jump, over the Shannon. It was done in a second; and, when she alighted on the distant bank, she kicked up her heels, and flung Larry on the soft turf.

No sooner was Larry thus planted than he looked her straight in the face, and cried out:—

"By my word, well done! That was not a bad leap, *for a calf!*"

She gazed at him for a moment, and then, assuming her own shape, said:—

"Larry Hoolahan, you are a bold fellow! Will you go back the way you came?"

"And that's what I will!" said he, "if you'll let me!"

So she changed to a calf again, and Larry got on her back. At another bound they were standing inside the Fairy Ring.

Then the Queen, once more assuming her own shape, addressed him.

"You have shown so much courage, Larry Hoolahan," said she, "that while you keep herds on this hill, you shall not be molested by me or mine. The day dawns. Go down to the farmer, and tell him this. And, if anything I can do will be of service to you, ask and you shall have it."

She vanished accordingly, and kept her word in never visiting the hill during Larry's lifetime; but he never troubled her with requests. He piped, and ate and drank at the farmer's expense, and roosted in the chimney-corner, occasionally casting an eye on the herd. He died at last; and is buried in a green valley of pleasant Tipperary. But whether the Fairies returned to the hill after his death is more than I can say.

THE WOOD-LADY

From Bohemia

Once upon a time there was a little girl named Betty. Her mother was a widow and very poor, and owned only a tumble-down house and two goats. Nevertheless, Betty was always cheerful. From Spring to Autumn she pastured the goats in the birch wood. Every morning when she left home, her mother gave her a little basket in which were a slice of bread and a spindle.

"My child," she said, "work hard to-day and fill the spindle before you return."

And, as Betty had no distaff, she wound the flax around her head, took the basket, and, with a skip and a jump, led her goats to the birch wood. There she sat under a tree and drew fibres of the flax from her head with her left hand, and let down the spindle with her right, so that it just hummed over the ground. And all the while she sang merrily, and the goats nibbled the green grass.

When the sun showed that it was midday she put aside her work, called her goats, and, after giving them each a morsel of bread, bounded into the wood to look for strawberries. When she came back she ate her fruit and bread, and, folding her hands, danced and sang. The goats, enjoying themselves among the green grass, thought: "What a merry shepherdess we have!" After her dance, she spun again. And at evening she drove her goats home, and her mother never had to scold her for bringing the spindle back empty.

One lovely Spring day, just as Betty sprang up to dance, suddenly—where she came, there she came!—a beautiful maiden stood before her. She wore a white dress as thin as gossamer, golden hair flowed to her waist, and on her head was a garland of wood flowers. Betty was struck dumb with astonishment.

The maiden smiled at her, and said in a very sweet voice:—

16

"Betty, are you fond of dancing?"

When the maiden spoke so prettily, Betty's terror quitted her, and she answered:—

"Oh! I should like to dance all day!"

"Come, then, let us dance together. I will teach you," said the maiden.

And she took Betty by the waist, and began to dance with her.

As they circled, such delicious music sounded over their heads that Betty's heart skipped within her. The musicians sat on branches of the birches. They were clad in black, ash-coloured, and variegated coats. They were choice musicians who had come together at the call of the beautiful maiden—nightingales, larks, linnets, goldfinches, thrushes, blackbirds, and a very skillful mocking-bird. Betty's cheeks flamed, her eyes glittered, she forgot her task and her goats. She could only gaze at her partner, who whirled her around with the most charming movements, and so lightly that the grass did not bend beneath her delicate weight.

They danced from noon till eve, and Betty's feet were neither weary nor sore. Then the beautiful maiden stopped, the music ceased, and as she came, so she went, and she vanished as if the earth had swallowed her.

Betty looked about. The sun had set. She clapped her hands to the top of her head, and remembered that her spindle was by no means full. She took the flax and put it with the spindle into her basket, and drove the goats home. That night her mother did not ask to see her work.

Next morning Betty again drove the goats to pasture. All happened as before. Where she came, there she came!—and the beautiful maiden seized Betty by the waist, and they danced from noon till eve.

Then Betty saw that the sun was setting and her spindle nearly empty, so she began to cry. But the maiden put her hands to Betty's head, took off the flax, and twined it round the stem of a slender birch, and began to spin. The spindle just swung over the ground. It grew fuller and fuller, and before the sun set behind the wood, all the yarn was spun. Giving the full spindle into Betty's hands, the maiden said:—

> *"Reel and grumble not!*
> *Reel and grumble not!"*

And as she came, so she went, and she vanished as if the ground had swallowed her. Betty drove the goats home, and gave her mother the full spindle.

Well, the next day all happened as before. Where she came, there she came!—and the beautiful maiden seized Betty by the waist, and they danced from noon to eve. then the maiden handed Betty a covered basket, saying:—

> *"Peep not, but go home!*
> *Peep not, but go home!"*

And as she came, so she went, and she vanished as if the ground had swallowed her.

At first Betty was afraid to peep into the basket, but when she was halfway home, she could not restrain herself. She lifted the cover and peeped, and, oh! how disappointed she was when she saw that the basket was full of birch leaves! She began to cry, and threw out two handfuls of the leaves, and was going to shake them all out of the basket, but she thought to herself: "They'll make good litter for the goats."

When she reached home her mother was waiting for her at the door.

"What sort of a spindle did you bring home to me yesterday?" cried she. "After you left this morning I began to reel. I reeled and reeled, and the spindle remained full. One skein! two skeins! three skeins! and the spindle was yet full! 'What evil spirit has spun for you?' grumbled I; and at that instant the yarn vanished from the spindle. Tell me the meaning of this."

So Betty confessed how she had danced with the beautiful maiden who had given her the full spindle, and who had said: "Reel and grumble not."

"That was a Wood-Fairy!" cried her mother in astonishment. "About noon in the Springtime, the Wood-Ladies dance. Lucky for you that she did not tickle you to death! It's a pity that you did not tell me before, for I might have had a room full of yarn, if I had reeled and grumbled not."

Then Betty bethought herself of the basket of leaves. She lifted the cover and peeped in again.

"Look! Look! Mother!" she cried.

Her mother looked and clapped her hands. The birch leaves were turned to gold!

"She told me not to peep until I reached home," said Betty, "but I disobeyed and threw two handfuls of the leaves away."

"Lucky for you that you did not throw them all away!" exclaimed her mother.

The next morning they both went to the place where Betty had thrown out the leaves, but on the road lay nothing but birch leaves. However, the gold Betty had brought home was enough to make them rich. Her mother bought a fine house and garden. They had many cattle. Betty had handsome clothes, and she did not need to pasture the goats any more. But though she had everything she desired, nothing gave her so great delight as the dance with the Wood-Fairy. She often went to the birch wood hoping to see the beautiful maiden, but she never again set eyes upon her.

III. *Elfin Mounds and Fairy Hills*

MONDAY! TUESDAY!

From Ireland

There once lived a lad in old Ireland named Lusmore. He had a great hump on his back, and whenever he sat down he had to rest his chin on his knee for support. But, in spite of this, he was as happy a cricket, and used to go about the country with a sprig of Fairy-cap, or Foxglove, in his little straw hat. He went from house to house plaiting baskets out of rushes, and in that way he earned a living. And he was so merry that people always gave him a penny more than he asked.

One evening, he was returning from a distant town, and as he walked slowly on account of his hump, it grew dark before he could reach home. He came to an old mound by the side of the road, and, being tired, sat down on it to rest.

He had not been sitting there long when he heard strains of music, and many little voices singing sweetly. He laid his ear to the mound, and perceived that the music and singing came from inside it. And he could hear the words that the little voices were chanting over and over again:—

> *"Monday! Tuesday!*
> *Monday! Tuesday!*
> *Monday! Tuesday!"*

It was all so very sweet, that Lusmore listened with delight; but by and by he grew tired of hearing the same words sung over and over. He waited politely until the voices had finished their song, then he called:—

> *"And Wednesday!"*

20

The Fairies—for it was the singing of Fairies that he heard—
were so pleased with Lusmore's addition to their words, that
they pulled him right down through the top of the mound with
the speed of a whirlwind. And he went falling and twirling
round and round as light as a feather.

He found himself in a palace so bright that it dazzled his eyes.
Then all the Fairies stopped capering and dancing, and came
crowding around him. And one, wearing a crown, stepped forward and said:—

> "Lusmore! Lusmore!
> The hump that you wore,
> On your back is no more.
> Look down on the floor,
> And see it, Lusmore!"

And as these words were being said, Lusmore felt himself
grow so light and happy, that he could have bounded up to the
moon. And he saw his hump tumble off his back and roll on the
floor. Then the Fairies took his hands, and danced around him,
and as they did so he became dizzy and fell asleep.

When he opened his eyes it was broad daylight, and the sun
was shining, and the birds were singing, and cows and sheep
were grazing peacefully around him. He put his hand to his
hump. It was gone! And there he was, as tall, straight, and handsome as any other lad in Ireland. And, besides all that, he was
dressed in a full suit of beautiful clothes.

He went toward his home stepping out lightly, and jumping
high at every step, so full of joy was he. And as he passed his
neighbours, they hardly knew him without his hump, and
because he was so straight and handsome, and was dressed so
finely.

Now, in another village, not far away, lived a lad named Jack
Madden. He also had a great hump on his back. He was a peev-
ish, cunning creature, and liked to scratch and pinch all who
came near him.

When he heard how the Fairies had taken away Lusmore's
hump, he decided that he, too, would visit them. So one night
after darkness had fallen, he sat down on the mound all alone,

and waited. He had not been there long before he heard the music, and the sweet voices singing:—

> *"Monday! Tuesday!*
> *Monday! Tuesday!*
> *Monday! Tuesday!*
> *And Wednesday!"*

And as he was in a very great hurry to get rid of his hump, he did not wait for the Fairies to finish their song, but yelled out, thinking that two days were better than one:—

> *"And Thursday and Friday!"*

No sooner had the words left his lips, than he was taken up quickly, and whisked through the mound with terrific force. And the Fairies came crowding around him, screeching and buzzing with anger, and crying out:—

> *"Our song you have spoiled!*
> *Our song you have spoiled!*
> *Our song you have spoiled!"*

Then the one wearing the crown stepped forward, and said:—

> *"Jack Madden! Jack Madden!*
> *Your words came so bad in,*
> *That your life we will sadden!*
> *Here's two humps for Jack Madden!"*

And quick as a wink, twenty Fairies brought Lusmore's hump and clapped it down on Jack Madden's back, and there it was fixed as firmly as if nailed on with tenpenny nails.

Then out of the mound they kicked him. And when morning was come, he crept home with the two humps on his back—and he is wearing them still.

THE GREEDY OLD MAN

From Cornwall

L ong ago in Cornwall, on a hillock called "the Gump," there
was a Fairy Ring. Many a good old man or woman, on
moonlit nights, had seen the Fairies dancing there at their revels, and had been rewarded with gifts small but rich.

Now, there was one greedy old man, who, having heard his
neighbours tell of the Fairy Gold at the revels, decided to steal
some of the treasure. So on a moonlit night, when all was quiet,
he stole softly up to "the Gump."

As he drew near he heard delightful music, which seemed to
come from inside the hillock. The notes were now slow and
solemn, and now quick and gay, so that the old man had to weep
and laugh in one breath. Then before he knew it, he began to
dance to the Fairy measure. He was forced by some unseen
power to whirl round and round; but in spite of this he kept his
wits about him, and watched to see what would happen.

Suddenly there was a crashing sound, and a door in the
hillock opened. Instantly the old man saw that everything about
him was ablaze with coloured lights. Each blade of grass was
hung with tiny bright lamps, and every tree and bush was illuminated with stars.

Out of the opening in the hillock marched a band of Goblins,
as if to clear the way. Then came a number of Fairy musicians
playing on every kind of musical instrument. These were followed by troop after troop of Elfin soldiers, carrying waving
banners.

The soldiers arranged themselves in two files on either side of
the door; but the Goblins, much to the old man's disgust, placed
themselves close behind him. As they were no bigger than his
thumb, he thought to himself: "If they bother me, I can easily
step on them and crush them with my foot."

This vast array having disposed itself, next from the hillock came a crowd of Elfin servants carrying pitchers of silver and gold, and goblets cut out of diamonds, rubies, emeralds, and other precious stones. Servants followed bearing aloft gold and silver platters heaped high with the richest meats, pastries, candies, and glowing fruits. A number of Elfin boys, clad in crimson, then set out small tables made of ivory curiously carved, and the servants arranged the feast with order.

Then out of the hillock came crowding thousands and thousands of lovely winged Fairies clad in gossamer robes of every colour, like the rainbow.

The music suddenly changed to low, delicate notes, and the old man found that he was no longer forced to dance and whirl about. And as he stood still, the perfume of a thousand rich flowers filled the air, and the whole vast host of Fairies began to sing a song as clear and sweet as the tinkle of silver bells.

Then from the hillock issued forth line after line of Elfin boys dressed in green and gold, and behind them on an ivory throne, borne aloft by a hundred Fairies, came the King and Queen of Fairyland blazing with beauty and jewels.

The throne was placed upon the hillock, which immediately bloomed with lilies and roses. Before the King and Queen was set the most beautiful of all the little tables laden with gold and silver dishes and precious goblets. The Fairies took their places at the other tables, and began to feast with a will.

"Now," thought the old man, "my time is come! If only I can creep up, without being seen, to the Fairy King's table, I shall be able to snatch enough gold to make me rich for life."

And with his greedy mind set on this, he crouched down, and began very slowly to creep toward the throne. But he did not see that thousands of Goblins had cast fine threads about his body, and were holding the ends in their hands.

Trembling with greed, the old man crept closer and closer to the Fairy King and Queen. He took his hat from his head, and raised it carefully to cover the royal throne and table; and, as he did so, he heard a shrill whistle. Instantly his hand was fixed powerless in the air. Then, with a sudden crash, all became dark around him.

"Whirr! Whirr! Whirr!" and he heard as if a flight of bees were brushing past his ears, and suddenly, his body, from head to foot, was stabbed with pins and pinched with tweezers. Then he was thrown violently upon his back with his arms out-stretched; and his arms and legs were fastened to the ground with magic chains. His tongue seemed tied with cords so that he could not call out.

And as he lay there trembling with fright and pain, he felt as though swarms of insects were running over him. Then he saw standing on his nose a grinning Goblin. This little monster stamped and jumped with great delight; then making a fearful grimace, shouted:—

> "Away! Away!
> I smell the day!"

And on this, an army of Goblins, Fairies, and Elves, who were running up and down the old man's body, stabbing him with pins, and pinching him with tweezers, jumped quickly down, and rushed into the hillock; which closed immediately. And the old man saw the Fairies no more.

At length the sun rose and he found that he was tied to the ground with a myriad of gossamer webs, which were covered with dew-drops that glistened like diamonds in the sunlight.

He shook himself free, and got up. Wet, cold, ashamed, and pinched black and blue, he returned to his home. And you may be sure that he never again tried to steal the Fairy Gold.

LEGEND OF BOTTLE HILL

From Ireland

It was in the good old days, when the Little People were more frequently seen than they are in these unbelieving times, that a farmer, named Mick Purcell, rented a few acres of barren ground not far from the city of Cork.

Mick had a wife and seven children. They did all that they could to get on, which was very little, for the poor man had no child grown big enough to help him in his work; and all that the poor woman could do was to mind the children, milk the cow, boil the potatoes, and carry the eggs to market. So besides the difficulty of getting enough to eat, it was hard on them to pay the rent.

Well, they did manage to get along for a good while; but at last came a bad year, and the little field of oats was spoiled, and the chickens died of the pip, and the pig got the measles, and poor Mick found that he hadn't enough to pay half his rent.

"Why, then, Molly," said he, "what'll we do?"

"Wisha, then, mavourneen, what would you do but take the cow to the Fair of Cork, and sell her?" said she. "And Monday is Fair-day, so you must go to-morrow."

"And what'll we do when she's gone?" said Mick.

"Never a know I know, Mick, but sure God won't leave us without help. And you know how good He was to us when little Billy was sick, and we had nothing at all for him to take—that good doctor gentleman came riding past and asked for a drink of milk, and he gave us two shillings, and sent me things and a bottle for the child; and he came to see Billy and never left off his goodness until he was well."

"Oh, you are always hopeful, Molly, and I believe you are right, after all," Mick said, "so I won't be sorry for selling the cow. I'll go to-morrow, and you must put a needle and thread through my coat, for you know it's ripped under the arm."

26

Molly told him he should have everything right. And about twelve o'clock the next day he left her, after having promised not to sell his cow except for the highest penny.

He drove the beast slowly through a little stream that crossed the road under the walls of an old fort; and as he passed, he glanced his eyes on a pile of stones and an old elder tree that stood up sharply against the sky.

"Oh, then, if only I had half the Fairy money that is buried in yon fort, 'tisn't driving this cow I'd be now!" said he aloud.

Then he moved on after his beast. 'Twas a fine day, and the sun shone brightly, and after he had gone six miles, he came to that hill—Bottle Hill it is called now, but that was not the name of it then.

"Good morrow, Mick!" said a little voice, and with that a little man started up out of the hill.

"Good morrow, kindly," said Mick, and he looked at the stranger who was like a dwarf with a bit of an old wrinkled face, for all the world like a dried cauliflower; only he had a sharp red nose, red eyes, and white hair. His eyes were never quiet, but looked at everything; and it made Mick's blood run cold just to see them roll so rapidly from side to side.

In truth Mick did not like the little man's company at all, and he drove his cow somewhat faster; but the little man kept up with him. Out of the corner of his eye Mick could see that he moved over the road without lifting one foot after the other; and the poor fellow's heart trembled within him.

"Where are you going with that cow, honest man?" said the little man at last.

"To the Fair of Cork, then," said Mick, trembling even more at the shrill and piercing voice.

"Are you going to sell her?" asked the little man.

"Why, then, what else am I going for, but to sell her?"

"Will you sell her to me?"

Mick started. He was afraid to have anything to do with the little man, but he was more afraid to say no.

"I'll tell you what, I'll give you this bottle," said the little man, pulling a bottle from under his coat.

Mick looked at him and the bottle, and in spite of his terror he could not help bursting into a loud fit of laughter.

"Laugh if you will!" said the little man, "but I tell you that this bottle is better for you than all the money you will get for the cow at Cork—aye, than ten thousand times as much."

Mick laughed again. "Why, then," said he, "do you think I am such a fool as to give my good cow for a bottle—and an empty one, too! Indeed, then, I won't!"

"You'd better give me the cow, and take the bottle—you'll not be sorry for it," said the little man.

"Why, then, what would Molly say? I'd never hear the last of it! And how should I pay the rent? And what should we do without a penny of money?"

"When you go home, never mind if your wife is angry," answered the little man, "but quiet yourself, and make her sweep the room, and set the table in the middle of the floor, and spread the best cover on it. Then put the bottle on the ground, saying these words: 'Bottle, do your duty!' And you will see the end of it."

"And is this all?" said Mick.

"No more," said the stranger, forcing the bottle into Mick's hand. Then he moved swiftly off after the cow.

Well, Mick, rather sick at heart, retraced his steps toward his cabin, and as he went he could not help turning his head to look after the little man; but he had vanished completely.

"He can't belong to this earth," exclaimed Mick in horror to himself. "But where is the cow?" She, too, was gone; and Mick hurried homeward muttering prayers and holding fast the bottle.

He soon reached his cabin, and surprised his wife sitting over the turf fire in the big chimney.

"Oh! Mick, are you come back?" said she. "Sure you weren't at Cork all the way? What has happened to you? Where is the cow? Did you sell her? How much money did you get for her? What news have you? Tell us everything."

"Why, then, Molly, if you'll give me time, I'll tell you all about it!"

"Oh! then, you sold her. Where's the money?"

"Arrah! stop a while, Molly, and I'll tell you all about it!"

"But what is that bottle under your waistcoat?" said Molly, seeing its neck sticking out.

"Why, then, be easy about it," said Mick, "till I tell it you." And putting the bottle on the table, he added, "That's all I got for the cow."

His poor wife was thunderstruck. She sat crying, while Mick told her his story, with many a crossing and blessing between him and harm. She could not help believing him, for she had great faith in Fairies. So she got up, and, without saying a word, began to sweep the earthen floor with a bunch of heather. Then she tidied everything, and put the long table in the middle of the room, and spread over it a clean cloth.

And then Mick, placing the bottle on the ground, said: "Bottle, do your duty!"

"Look! Look there, mammy!" cried his eldest son. "Look there! Look there!" and he sprang to his mother's side, as two tiny fellows rose like light from the bottle; and in an instant they covered the table with dishes and plates of gold and silver, full of the finest victuals that ever were seen. And when all was done, the two tiny fellows went into the bottle again.

Mick and his wife looked at everything with astonishment; they had never seen such dishes and plates before, and the very sight of them almost took their appetites away. But at length Molly said:—

"Come and sit down, Mick, and try to eat a bit. Sure, you ought to be hungry, after such a good day's work!"

So they all sat down at the table. After they had eaten as much as they wished, Molly said:—

"I wonder will these two good, little gentlemen carry away these fine things."

They waited, but no one came; so Molly put the dishes and plates carefully aside. The next day Mick went to Cork and sold some of them, and bought a horse and cart.

Weeks passed by, and the neighbours saw that Mick was making money; and, though he and his wife did all they could to keep the bottle a secret, their landlord soon found out about it. Then he took the bottle by force away from Mick, and carried it carefully home.

As for Mick and his wife, they had so much money left that the loss of the bottle did not worry them much at first; but they

kept on spending their wealth as if there was no end to it. And
to make a long story short, they became poorer and poorer, until
they had to sell their last cow.

So one morning early, Mick once more drove his cow to the
Fair of Cork. It was hardly daybreak when he left home, and he
walked on until he reached the big hill; and just as he got to its
top, and cast his eyes before and around him, up started the
little man out of the hill.

"Well, Mick Purcell," said he, "I told you that you would be a
rich man!"

"Indeed, then, so I was, that is no lie for you, sir," replied
Mick. "But it's not rich I am now! And if you happen to have
another bottle, here is the cow for it."

"And here is the bottle!" said the little man, smiling. "You
know what to do with it."

And with that both the cow and the stranger disappeared as
they had done before.

Mick hurried away, anxious to get home with the bottle. He
arrived with it safely enough, and called out to Molly to put
the room to rights; and to lay a clean cloth on the table. Which
she did.

Mick set the bottle on the ground, and cried out: "Bottle, do
your duty!"

In a twinkling two great, stout men with two huge clubs,
issued from the bottle, and belaboured poor Mick and his family until they lay groaning on the floor. Then the two men went
into the bottle again.

Mick, as soon as he came to himself, got up and looked
around him. He thought and he thought. He lifted up his wife
and children, then leaving them to recover as best they could,
he put the bottle under his arm, and went to visit his landlord.

The landlord was having a great feast, and when he saw that
Mick had another bottle, he invited him heartily to come in.

"Show us your bottle, Mick," said he.

So Mick set it on the floor, and spoke the proper words; and
in a moment the landlord tumbled to the floor, and all his guests
were running, and roaring, and sprawling, and kicking, and
shrieking, while the two great, stout men belaboured them well.

"Stop those two scoundrels, Mick Purcell," shouted the landlord, "or I'll hang you!"

"They shall never stop," said Mick, "till I get my own bottle that I see on top of yon shelf."

"Give it to him! Give it to him, before we are killed!" cried the landlord.

Mick put his old bottle in his bosom. Then the two great, stout men jumped into the new one, and Mick carried both bottles safely home.

And to make my story short, from that time on Mick prospered. He got richer than ever, and his son married the landlord's daughter. And both Mick and his wife lived to a great old age. They died on the same day, and at their wake the servants broke both bottles. But the hill has the name upon it; for so it will always be Bottle Hill to the end of the world, for this is a strange story.

IV. Little Men and Treasures of Gold

THE BOY WHO FOUND
THE POTS OF GOLD

From Ireland

There was once a poor boy who used to drive his cart along the road, and sell turf to the neighbours. He was a strange boy, very silent, and spent his evenings in his little hut, where he lived alone, reading old bits of books he had picked up in his rambles. And as he read, he longed to be rich and live in a fine house with a garden all round him, and to have plenty of books.

Now he once read how the Fairies' Shoemakers, the Leprechauns—merry, tricksy little sprites—sit at sunset under the hedges mending the shoes of Elfin Folk. And how they chuckle as they work, for they know where the pots of Fairy Gold are hidden.

So, evening after evening, the boy watched the hedges hoping to catch a glimpse of a little cobbler, and to hear the click-clack of his tiny hammer.

At last, one evening, just as the sun was setting, the boy saw a little Leprechaun sitting under a dock-leaf, and working away hard on a small boot. He was dressed in green and wore a red cap on his head. The boy jumped down from his cart, and catching the Leprechaun by the neck, cried merrily:—

"Ho! Ho! My fine little man, you can't get away until you tell me where the Fairy Gold is hidden!"

"Easy now!" said the little man, laughing. "Don't hurt me, and I'll tell you all about it. I could harm you, if I wished, for I have the power; but I like you, and you are an industrious lad. So carry me to yonder fort, and I'll show you the gold."

Carrying the Leprechaun carefully, the boy took a few steps,

32

and found himself close to the ruins of an old fort. A door opened in a stone wall, and he walked in.

"Now look around," said the Leprechaun.

Then the boy saw that the whole ground was covered with gold pieces, while pots full of gold and silver money stood about in such plenty that it seemed as if all the riches of the world were there.

"Take what you want," said the Leprechaun, "and be quick about it; for if the door shuts you will never leave this place alive."

The boy hurried, and gathered his arms full of gold and silver, and hastening out of the door, flung all into the cart. Then he brought out some of the pots; but when he was on his way back for more, the door shut with a clap like thunder, and night fell, and all was dark.

The boy saw no more of the Leprechaun; and as he could not even thank him, he thought that it was best to drive home at once and hide his treasure.

When he reached his hut, he counted all the bright yellow pieces and shining silver ones, and found that he was as rich as a king. And because he was wise, he told no one about his adventure, but the next day drove to town and put all his money in the bank.

After that he ordered a fine house, and laid out a spacious garden, and had servants, and carriages, and many books. Then he married the daughter of a magistrate, and became great and powerful. His memory is still held in reverence by his townspeople. His descendants are living rich and happy; and no matter how much they give to the poor, their wealth always increases.

The Ragweed

From Ireland

Tom was as clean, clever, and tight looking a lad as any in the whole county Cork. One fine holiday in harvest-time, he was taking a ramble and was sauntering along the sunny side of a hedge, when suddenly he heard a crackling sound among the leaves.

"Dear me!" said he, "but isn't it really surprising to hear the stone-chats singing so late in the season!"

And with that he stole along, going on the tips of his toes, to see if he could get sight of what was making the noise. He looked sharply under the bushes, and what should he see in a nook in the hedge but a big brown pitcher holding a gallon or more of dark looking liquor. And standing close to it was a little, diny, dony bit of an old man as big as your thumb, with a tiny cocked hat stuck on the top of his head, and a deesy, daushy, leather apron hanging down before him.

The little old man pulled a little brown stool from under the hedge, and, standing upon it, dipped a little cup into the pitcher. Then he took the cup out, full of the brown liquor, and putting it on the ground, sat down on the stool under the shadow of the pitcher. He began to put a heel-piece on a bit of a boot just the size for himself.

"Bless my soul!" said Tom to himself, in great surprise, "I've often heard tell of the Leprechauns, but I never rightly believed in them! But here's one in real earnest! Now if I set about things right, I'm a made man! Folks say that a body must never take his eyes off them or they'll get away."

So Tom stole nearer, with his eyes fixed on the little man, just as a cat does with a mouse. And when he got close up to him, he said softly:—

"How goes your work, neighbour?"

The little man raised his head. "Very well, thank you kindly," said he.

"I'm surprised that you should be working on a holiday," said Tom.

"That's my own business, not yours," said the little man.

"Well, will you be civil enough to tell me what's in your pitcher?" said Tom.

"That I will, with pleasure," said the little man. "'Tis Elfin beer."

"Elfin beer!" said Tom. "Thunder and fire! Where did you get it?"

"Why I made it—I made it of heath," said the little man.

"Of heath!" said Tom bursting out laughing. "And will you give a body a taste of it?" asked he.

"I'll tell you what it is, young man," said the Leprechaun, "it would be fitter for you to be looking after your cows that have broken into the oats yonder, than to stand here asking honest folks foolish questions!"

Tom was so taken by surprise at this, that he was just going to turn his head to look for the cows, when he remembered not to take his eyes off the Leprechaun. Instead he made a grab at the little man and caught him up in his hand; but, as bad luck would have it, he overturned the pitcher with his foot, and all the liquor was spilt.

"You little rogue!" cried he, shaking the Leprechaun hard, and looking very wicked and angry. "Tell me where your gold is hidden, and show me all your money!"

At that the little man was quite frightened. "Come along with me," said he, "and I'll show you a crock of gold in a field over there."

So they went, Tom holding the Leprechaun very tightly, and never taking his eyes off him. They crossed hedges and ditches and a crooked bit of bog, until they came to a great field of ragweed. Then the Leprechaun pointed to one of the weeds, and said:—

"Dig under that, and you'll get a crock full of guineas."

As Tom had no spade with him, he thought to himself: "I'll run home and fetch one. And so that I'll know the place again, I'll tie my garter around this weed."

So he tied his red garter around the ragweed.

"I suppose," said the Leprechaun politely, "that now you have no further use for me."

"No," said Tom, "you may go, if you wish. And thank you very kindly," he said, laughing loudly, "for showing me where all your money lies!"

"Well, good-bye to you, Tom," said the little man, "and much good may it do you, what you'll get," said he; and with that he jumped behind the weed, and vanished.

So Tom ran home for dear life and fetched a spade, and then back as hard as he could go to the field.

But when he got there, lo, and behold! not a ragweed in the whole field but had a red garter, just like his own, tied to it! And as for digging up that whole field, it was out of the question, for there were more than forty good Irish acres in it.

So Tom went home again with his spade, a little cooler, and, you may be sure, ashamed to tell any one about the neat turn the Leprechaun had served him.

The Bad Boy and
the Leprechaun

From Ireland

Now, it is well known that if a Leprechaun is offended he can be most malicious. So one must treat him politely, or he will not reveal where the pots of Fairy Gold are hidden.

It happened one afternoon that a lad was working in the fields when he heard at his feet, "Rip! Rap! Tick! Tack!" and looking down he saw a little fellow no bigger than his hand sitting under a burdock-leaf, mending shoes. He grabbed him up, and putting him in his pocket, ran home. There was no one in the house, so he tied the Leprechaun to the hob, saying:—

"Tell me, you little rogue, where I may find a pot of gold."

"That I will not tell you," replied the Leprechaun, "unless you let me go, so that I may finish cobbling the Elfin King's shoes."

"I'll make you tell me *now* where the gold is!" said the lad.

And with that he built a rousing fire under the Leprechaun to roast him.

"Oh, take me off! Take me off!" yelled the little fellow, "and I'll tell you! Just go to the burdock-leaf under which I was sitting, and there is the pot of gold. Only go, dig, and find it, before the sun sets."

The lad was so delighted that, without stopping to untie the Leprechaun, he ran out of the house. It happened that his mother was just coming in with a pail of new milk. He hit the pail and spilt the milk on the floor, but he ran on laughing. And when his mother saw the Leprechaun struggling on the hob, she was furiously angry.

"See what bad luck you have brought us, you rogue!" she cried. And with that she untied the little fellow and kicked him out of the house.

But the lad ran on until he came to the burdock-leaf; and he dug, and dug, and dug, but there was no pot of gold there, for the sun had set. So he started sorrowfully for home, and just as he was passing an old fort he heard laughter, and a squeaky voice crying out:—

"That boy is looking for a pot of gold! ha! ha! But little does he know that a whole crock full is lying at the bottom of the old quarry. Only he must go to fetch it at midnight, and he must not take his mother with him."

When the lad heard this he hurried home and told his mother. At midnight he started out, after ordering her to stay in the house. But as soon as he was gone she thought to herself: "I'll get to the quarry before he does, and find and keep the gold!"

So she ran by a shorter way, and when she reached the edge of the quarry she slipped on a stone, fell to the bottom, and broke her leg. And there she lay groaning dreadfully.

Soon the lad came along, and just as he was going to climb down he heard some one groan.

"What's below?" he cried in a fright. "Is it evil? Is it good?"

"It's your mother with a broken leg," groaned she.

"And is this my pot of gold!" exclaimed the lad, angrily.

And with that he ran for a neighbour, and together they drew the woman up and took her home. And from that day on she was lame.

As for the Leprechaun, he is still sitting under the burdock-leaf, and he laughs at the lad and his mother, as he mends his little shoes with his tiny hammer, Rip! Rap! Tick! Tack!—but they are afraid to touch him, for they know he can punish them badly.

THE KNOCKERS' DIAMONDS

From Cornwall

JACK THE TINNER'S STORY

One night I was working away for dear life, in yonder old tin mine. I was in good heart, because at every stroke of my tool I heard three or four clicks from Knockers who were working ahead. By the sounds they seemed to be very near.

Just then a hard stroke of my pick broke open the rock in front of me, and I saw into a large grotto. The light of my candle fell on its walls, and my eyes were dazzled by the glistening of bunches of diamonds and crystals of all colours that hung down from the roof, and encrusted the sides.

While I was rubbing my eyes, I saw three little Knockers. They were no bigger than sixpenny dolls, yet their faces were old and strange. The eldest one was sitting on a stone, his jacket off, and his shirt-sleeves rolled up. Between his knees he held a tiny anvil, and he was sharpening a borer about the size of a needle, for one of the Knockers. The third little fellow was awaiting his turn, pick-axe in hand.

When the Knocker-smith had finished sharpening the borer, he rested his hammer on the anvil, and looked toward me.

"What cheer, comrade?" he said. "I could not think from where the cold wind was coming. The draught from your hole has blown out my light."

"Oh! Good-morning! Is that you? How are you?" said I. "And how is the rest of your family? I am glad to see you. I'll fetch you my candle in a minute, that you may see better. In fact, I'll give you a pound of candles, my dear, with all my heart, if you want them," said I.

In less than no time I put my hand through the hole to give

him my candle, when, what do you think?—there wasn't a Knocker in sight!

"Where are they gone?" thought I. Then I heard them somewhere in the lode ahead, tee-heeing, and cackling, and squeaking like young rabbits.

And there I was left in their pretty workshop, with bunches of diamonds all around me. I laid my coat on the floor, and filled it with diamonds and coloured crystals, and then hurried out of the mine. But when I went back to get some more, the rocks had caved in, and I never could find the grotto again.

Skillywidden

From Cornwall

Every one knows that before King Arthur ruled in Britain, the Danes conquered Cornwall. Then many of the rich Cornish folk buried their gold and treasures, and fled to the land of Wales. A few years after that King Arthur came with his knights, and drove the Danes out of Cornwall. Then the folk came back, but never again could they find their buried treasures. And to-day none but the Spriggans know where the gold is hidden.

Well, one morning not very long ago Uncle Billy of Trevidga was out on the side of a hill, cutting away the furze that was as high as his head, with bare places here and there covered with white clover, heath, and whortleberries. Uncle Billy was working hard, when he spied the prettiest little creature, a real little man, not bigger than a kitten, sleeping on a bank of wild thyme. He was dressed in a green coat, sky-blue breeches, and diamond-buckled shoes. His tiny cocked hat was drawn over his face, to shade it from the sun.

Uncle Billy stooped and looked at him, and longed to carry him home to his children, for he had a houseful of little ones, boys and girls. So he took off his cuff, and slipped it quickly over the Spriggan—for a Spriggan it was that lay there—before he could wake.

The little fellow opened his pretty eyes, and said in a sleepy voice: "Mammy! Where are you? Mammy! Daddy!" Then he saw Uncle Billy looking at him. "Who are you?" he said. "You're a fine, great giant! I want my Mammy! Can you find her for me?"

"I do not know where she is," answered Uncle Billy. "But come home with me, and play with my children, until your Mammy finds you."

"Very well," said the Spriggan. "I love to ride goats over the

41

rocks, and to have milk and blackberries for supper. Will you give me some?"

"Yes, my son," said Uncle Billy; and with that he picked up the Spriggan gently, and carried him home.

Well, you should have seen the children! They were so happy to own a Spriggan! They set the little fellow on the hearth, and he played with them as if he had known them always. Uncle Billy and his wife were delighted, and the children shouted for joy, when the pretty little man capered and jumped about. They called him Bobby Spriggan. Twice a day they gave him a wee mug of milk and a few blackberries, and now and then some haws for a change.

In the mornings, while Uncle Billy's wife and the children were doing the housework, Bobby Spriggan sat perched on the faggots in the woodcorner, and sang and chirped away like a Robin Redbreast.

When the hearth was swept, and the kitchen made tidy, and Uncle Billy's wife was knitting, Bobby would dance for hours on the hearthstone. The faster her needles clicked, the faster he danced and spun around and around. And the children laughed and clapped their hands, and danced with him.

A week or so after Bobby Spriggan had been found, Uncle Billy had to leave home. As he wished to keep the little fellow safe and sound until he told where the crocks of Cornish gold were hidden, Uncle Billy shut him up with the youngest children in the barn, and put a strong padlock on the door.

"Now stay in the barn and play," called Uncle Billy to the children. "And don't try to get out, or when I come home you'll get a walloping," said he, and then went away.

The children laughed a part of the time, and a part of the time they cried, for they did not like to be locked in the barn. But Bobby Spriggan was as merry as a cricket. He danced and sang, and peeped through the cracks in the wall at the men who were working in the fields. And when the men went to dinner, up jumped Bobby and unbarred a window.

"Come along, children!" he cried. "Now for a game of hide-and-seek in the furze!"

Then he sprang out the window, and the children followed after. And away they all ran to play in the furze.

They were shouting and throwing whortleberries about, when suddenly they saw a little man and woman no bigger than Bobby. The little man was dressed like Bobby, except that he wore high riding-boots with silver spurs. The little woman's green gown was spangled with glittering stars. Diamond shoe-buckles shone on her high-heeled shoes, and her tiny steeple-crowned hat was perched on a pile of golden curls, wreathed with heath blossoms. The pretty little soul was weeping and wringing her hands, and crying:—

"O my dear, tender Skillywidden! Where canst thou be! Shall I never set eyes on thee again, my only one, my only joy?"

"Go back! Go back!" cried Bobby Spriggan to the children. Then he called out: "Here I am, Mammy!"

And just as he said, "Here I am," the little man and the little woman, and Bobby Spriggan himself, who was their precious Skillywidden, vanished, and were seen no more.

The children cried and cried, and went home. And when Uncle Billy came back you may be sure that he whipped them all soundly. And it served them right, for if they had minded and stayed in the barn, Bobby Spriggan would have shown Uncle Billy where the Cornish gold was hidden.

V. Glad Little, Sad Little, Bad Little Elves

LITTLE REDCAP

From Ireland

Sure and it was in old Ireland, some years ago, that Tom Coghlan returned one evening to his house, expecting to find the fire blazing, the potatoes boiling, and his wife and children as merry as grigs. But, instead, the fire was out, his wife was scolding, and the children were all crying from hunger.

Poor Tom was quite astonished to find matters going on so badly, for, though there was a plenty of potatoes in the house, there wasn't a single stick of wood for the fire. Something had to be done. And Tom bethought himself of the great furze-bushes that grew around the ruins of the old fort on top of the near-by hill. So he snatched up his axe and away he went.

Before he reached the top of the hill the sun had gone down, and the moon had risen and was shedding her wavering, watery light on the ruins of the old fort. The breeze rustled the dark furze-bushes with an eerie sound, and Tom shivered with dread. But he braced up his heart, and, approaching the fort, raised his axe to cut down a big bush. Just then, near him, he heard the shriek of a small, shrill voice.

Tom, startled, let the axe fall from his grasp, and, looking up, saw perched on the furze-bush in front of him a little old man, not more than a foot and a half high. He wore a red cap. His face was the colour of a withered mushroom, while his sparkling eyes, twinkling like diamonds in the dark, illuminated his distorted face. His thin legs dangled from his fat, round body.

"Ho! Ho!" said the Little Redcap, "is that what you're after, Tom Coghlan? What did me and mine ever do to you that you should cut down our bushes?"

"Why, then, nothing at all, your honour!" said Tom, recovering a bit from his fright, "nothing at all! Only the children were crying from hunger, and I thought I'd make bold to cut a bush or two to boil the potatoes, for we haven't a stick in the house."

"You mustn't cut down these bushes, Tom!" said the Little Redcap. "But, as you are an honest man, I'll buy them from you, though I have a better right to them than you have. So, if you'll take my advice, carry this mill home with you, and let the bushes alone," said the Little Redcap, holding out a tiny stone mill for grinding meal.

"Mill, indeed!" said Tom, looking with astonishment at the thing, which was so small that he could have put it with ease into his breeches pocket. "Mill, indeed! And what good will a bit of a thing like that do me? Sure, it won't boil the potatoes for the children!"

"What good will it do you?" said the Little Redcap. "I'll tell you what good it will do you! It will make you and your family as fat and strong as so many stall-fed bullocks. And if it won't boil the potatoes, it will do a great deal better, for you have only to grind it, and it will give you the greatest plenty of elegant meal. But if you ever sell any of the meal, that moment the mill will lose its power."

"It's a bargain," said Tom. "So give me the mill, and you're heartily welcome to the bushes."

"There it is for you, Tom," said the Little Redcap, throwing the mill down to him; "there it is for you, and much good may it do you! But remember you are not to sell the meal on any account."

"Let me alone for that!" said Tom.

And then he made the best of his way home, where his wife was trying to comfort the children, wondering all the time what in the world was keeping Tom. And when she saw him return without so much as one stick of wood to boil the potatoes, her anger burst out. But Tom soon quieted her by placing the mill on the table and telling her how he had got it from the Little Redcap.

"We'll try it directly," said she. And they pulled the table into the middle of the floor, and commenced grinding away with the mill. Before long a stream of beautiful meal began pouring from it; and in a short time they had filled every dish and pail in the house. Tom's wife was delighted, as you may believe, and the children managed the best they could for that night by eating plenty of raw meal.

Well, after that everything went very well with Tom and his family. The mill gave them all the meal they wanted, and they grew as fat and sleek as coach-horses. But one morning when Tom was away from home, his wife needed money. So she took a few pecks of the meal to town and sold it in the market.

And sorry enough she was, for that night, when Tom came home and began to grind the mill, not a speck of meal would come from it! He could not for the life of him find out the reason, for his wife was afraid to tell him about her selling the meal.

"Sure, and the little old fellow cheated me well!" thought Tom, as mad as a nest of hornets. So he put his axe under his arm, and away he went to the old fort, determined to punish the Little Redcap by cutting down his bushes. But scarcely had he lifted his axe, when the Little Redcap appeared, and mighty angry he was, too, that Tom should come cutting his bushes, after having made a fair bargain with him.

"You deceitful, little, ugly vagabond!" cried Tom, flourishing his axe, "to give me a mill that wasn't worth a sixpence! If you don't give me a good one for it, I'll cut down every bush!"

"What a blusterer you are, Tom!" said the Little Redcap, "but you'd better be easy and let the bushes alone, or maybe you'll pay for it! Deceive you, indeed! Didn't I tell you that mill would lose its power if you sold any of the meal?"

"And sure and I didn't, either," said Tom.

"Well, it's all one for that," answered the Little Redcap, "for if you didn't, your wife did. And as to giving you another mill, it's out of the question. For the one I gave you was the only one in the fort. And a hard battle we had to get it away from another party of the Good People! But I'll tell you what I'll do with you, Tom; let the bushes alone, and I'll make a doctor of you."

"A doctor, indeed!" said Tom. "Maybe it's a fool you're making of me!"

But it was no such thing, for the Little Redcap gave Tom Coghlan a charm so that he could cure any sick person. And Tom took it home, and became a great man with a very full purse. He gave good schooling to his children. One of them he made a grand butter-merchant in the city of Cork, and the youngest son—being ever and always a well-spoken lad—he made a lawyer; and his two daughters married well.

And Tom is as happy as a man can be!

THE CURMUDGEON'S SKIN

From Ireland

It is well known in old Ireland that a Four-leaved Shamrock has the power to open a man's eyes so that he can see all kinds of enchantments, and this is what happened to Billy Thompson:—

One misfortune after another decreased his goods. His sheep died; and his pig got the measles, so that he was obliged to sell it for little or nothing. But still he had his cow.

"Well," said Billy to his wife, for he was a good-humoured fellow, and always made the best of things,—"Well!" said he, "it can't be helped! Anyhow, we'll not want the drop of milk to our potatoes, as long as the cow's left to comfort us!"

The words were hardly out of his mouth when a neighbour came running up to tell him that his cow had fallen from a cliff, and was lying dead in the Horses' Glen. For Billy, you must know, had sent his cow that very morning to graze on the cliff.

"Och! Ullagone!" cried Billy. "What'll we do now! Och! you cruel, unnatural beast as to clift yourself, when you knowed as well as myself that we couldn't do without you at all! For sure enough now the children will be crying for the drop of milk to their potatoes!"

Such was Billy's lament, as with a sorrowful heart he made the best of his way to the Horses' Glen. "Anyway," thought he, "I'll skin the carcass, and the meat will make fine broth for the children."

It took him some time to find where the poor beast was lying, but at last he did find her, all smashed to pieces at the foot of a big rock. And he began to skin her as fast as he could, but having no one to help him, by the time the job was finished, the sun had gone down.

Now Billy was so intent on his work that he did not perceive the lapse of time, but when he raised his head and saw the darkness coming on, and listened to the murmuring wind, all the tales he had ever heard of the Pooka, the Banshee, and Little Redcap, the mischievous Fairy, floated through his mind, and made him want to get home as fast as possible. He snatched a tuft of grass, wiped his knife, and seized hold of the hide.

It so happened that in the little tuft of grass with which Billy wiped his knife was a Four-leaved Shamrock. And whether from grief or fear, Billy, instead of throwing away the grass, put it in his pocket along with his knife. And when he stood up and turned to take a last look at the carcass he saw, instead of his poor cow, a little old Curmudgeon sitting bolt upright, looking as if he had just been skinned alive!

"Billy Thompson! Billy Thompson," cried the little old fellow in a shrill, squeaking voice. "You spalpeen! You'd better come back with my skin! A pretty time of day we've come to, when a gentleman like me cannot take a bit of sleep but a rude fellow must come and strip the hide off him! But you'd better bring it back, Billy Thompson, or I'll make you remember how you dared to skin me, you spalpeen!"

Now Billy, though he was greatly frightened, remembered that he had a black-handled knife in his pocket, and whoever has that, 'tis said, can look all the Fairies of the world in the face without quaking. So he put his hand on the knife, and began backing away, with the skin under his arm.

"Why, then, your honour," said he, "if it's this skin you're wanting, you must know it's the skin of my poor cow that was clifted yonder there. And sore and sorrowful the children will be for the want of her little drop of milk!"

"Why, then, if that's what you'd be after, Billy, my boy," said the little fellow, at the same time jumping before him with the speed of a greyhound, "do you think I'm such a fool as to let you walk off with my skin? If you don't drop it in the turn of a hand, you'll sup sorrow!"

"Nonsense!" said Billy, drawing out his black-handled knife, and holding it so the little man could see it. "Never a one of me will let you have this skin till you give me back my cow. I know well enough she was not clifted at all, at all, and that you and the other Curmudgeons have got hold of her!"

"You'd better keep a civil tongue in your head," said the little fellow, who seemed to get quite soft at the sight of the knife.

"But you're a brave boy, Billy Thompson, and I've taken a fancy to you! I don't say but I might get you your cow again, if you'll give me back my skin."

"Thank you, kindly," said Billy, winking slyly. "Give me the cow first; then I will."

"Well, there she is for you, you unbelieving hound!" said the little Curmudgeon.

And for sure and for certain, what did Billy Thompson hear but his own cow bellowing behind him for the bare life! And when he looked back what should he see but his cow running over rocks and stones with a long rope hanging to one of her legs, and four little fellows, with red caps on them, hunting her as fast as they could!

"There'll be a battle for her, Billy! There'll be a battle!" laughed the little Curmudgeon.

And sure enough, the little Redcaps began to fight, and in the meantime the cow, finding herself at liberty, ran towards Billy, who lost not a minute, but, throwing the skin on the ground, seized the cow by the tail and began to drive her away.

"Not so fast, Billy!" said the little Curmudgeon, who stuck close by his side; "not so fast! Though I gave you the cow, I didn't give you the rope that's hanging to her leg."

"A bargain's a bargain," said Billy, "so as I've got it, I'll keep rope and all."

"If you say that again," said the little fellow, "I'll be after calling the Redcaps that are fighting below there. But I don't want to be too hard on you, Billy, for if you have a mind for the rope, I'll give it to you for the little tuft of grass you have in your pocket."

"There, take it," said Billy, throwing down the grass with the Four-leaved Shamrock in it.

No sooner was it out of his hand than he received such a blow that it dashed him to the ground, insensible. When he came to himself, the sun was shining, and where should he be but near his own house with the cow grazing beside him? Billy Thompson could hardly believe his eyes, and thought it was all a dream, till he saw the rope hanging to his cow's leg.

And that was a lucky rope for him! For, from that day out, his cow gave more milk than any six cows in the parish, and Billy began to look up in the world. He took farms, and purchased cattle till he became very rich. But no one could ever get him to go to the Horses' Glen. And today he never passes an old fort, or hears a blast of wind, without taking off his hat in compliment to the Good People; and 'tis only right that he should.

JUDY AND THE FAIRY CAT

From Ireland

Late one Hallowe'en an old woman was sitting up spinning. There came a soft knock at the door.

"Who's there?" asked she.

There was no answer, but another knock.

"Who's there?" she asked a second time.

Still no answer, but a third knock. At that the old woman got up in anger.

"Who's there?" she cried.

A small voice, like a child's, sobbed: "Ah, Judy dear, let me in! I am so cold and hungry! Open the door, Judy dear, and let me sit by the fire and dry myself! Judy dear, let me in! Oh—let—me—in!"

Judy, thinking that it must be a small child who had lost its way, ran to the door, and opened it. In walked a large Black Cat waving her tail, and two black kittens followed her. They walked deliberately across the floor, and sat down before the fire, and began to warm themselves and lick their fur, purring all the time. Judy never said a word, but closed the door, and went back to her spinning.

At last the Black Cat spoke.

"Judy dear," said she, "do not sit up so late. This is the Fairies' holiday, and they wish to hold a counsel in your kitchen, and eat their supper here. They are very angry because you are still up, and they cannot come in. Indeed, Judy, they are determined to kill you. Only for myself and my two daughters, you would now be dead. So take my advice and do not interfere with the Fairies' Hallowe'en. But give me some milk, for I must be off."

Well, Judy got up in a great fright and ran as fast as she could, and brought three saucers full of milk, and set them on the floor before the cats. They lapped up all the milk, then the Black Cat called her daughters and stood up.

"Thank you, Judy dear," she said. "You have been very civil to me, and I'll not forget. Good night! Good night!"

And with that she and her kittens whisked up the chimney, and were gone.

Then Judy saw something shining on the hearth. She picked it up; it was a piece of silver money, more than she could earn in a month. She put out the light, and went to bed; and never again did she sit up late on Hallowe'en and interfere with the Fairy hours.

THE BOGGART

From Yorkshire

Once upon a time a Boggart lived in a farmer's house. He was a mischievous Elf, and specially fond of teasing the children. When they were eating their supper, he would make himself invisible, and, standing back of their chairs, would snatch away their bread and butter and drain their mugs of milk. On cold nights he would pull the clothes from their warm beds and tickle their feet.

And the children liked to tease the Boggart in return. There was a closet in the kitchen with a large knot-hole in its wall behind which the Boggart lived. The children used to stick a shoehorn into the hole; and the Boggart would throw it back at them. The shoehorn made the little man so angry that one day he threw it at the youngest boy's head and hurt him badly.

At length the Boggart became such a torment that the farmer and his wife decided to move to another place and let the mischievous creature have their house to himself.

The day of the moving came. All the furniture was piled into a wagon, and a neighbour called to say good-bye. "So, farmer," said he, "you are leaving the old house at last!"

"Heigh-ho!" sighed the farmer, "I am forced to do it. That villain Boggart torments us so that we have no rest night or day! He almost killed my youngest boy. So you see we are forced to flit."

Scarcely were the words out of his mouth when a squeaky voice cried from the bottom of the churn, that was in the wagon:—

"Aye! Aye! We're flitting, you see!"

"Ods! Hang it!" cried the poor farmer. "There is that villain Boggart again! If he's going along with us, I shall not stir a peg. Nay! Nay! It's no use, Molly," said he turning to his wife. "We may as well stay here in the old house as to be tormented in the new one that is not so convenient!"

And they stayed.

OWNSELF

From Northumberland

Once upon a time there was a widow and her little boy. Their home was a small cottage in the wood. The mother worked hard from early morning until evening, and she was so tired that she liked to go to bed early. But the little boy did not like to go to bed early at all.

One evening when his mother told him to undress, he begged her, saying: "I'm not sleepy. May I sit up just this once?"

"Very well," said she. "Sit up if you wish, but if the Fairies catch you here alone, they will surely carry you off." Then she went to bed.

The little boy laughed, and sat down on the hearth before the fire, watching the blaze and warming his hands.

By and by he heard a giggling and a laughing in the chimney, and the next minute he saw a tiny girl, as big as a doll, come tumbling down and jump on to the hearth in front of him.

At first the little boy was dreadfully frightened, but the tiny girl began to dance so prettily, and to nod her head at him in such a friendly way, that he forgot to be afraid.

"What do they call you, little girl?" said he.

"My name is Ownself," said she proudly. "What is yours?"

"My name," he answered, laughing very hard, "is My Ownself."

Then the two children began to play together as if they had known each other all their lives. They danced, and they sang, and they roasted chestnuts before the fire, and they tickled the house-cat's ears. Then the fire commenced to flicker, and it grew dimmer and dimmer; so the little boy took the poker and stirred up the embers. And a hot coal tumbled out and rolled on to Ownself's tiny foot. And, oh! how she screamed! Then she wept, and flew into such a rage that the little boy got frightened and hid behind the door.

Just then a squeaky voice called down the chimney: "Ownself! Ownself! What wicked creature hurt you?"

"My Ownself! My Ownself!" she screamed back.

"Then come here, you troublesome little Fairy," cried the voice angrily.

And a Fairy mother, slipper in hand, came hurrying down the chimney; and catching Ownself, she whipped her soundly and carried her off, saying:—

"What's all this noise about, then? If you did it your ownself, there's nobody to blame but yourself!"

THE SICK-BED ELVES

From China

Wang Little-Third-One lay stretched on his bed of bamboo laths, where a low fever kept him. He complained to every one, especially to his friend the Magician who came to see him.

The Magician was very wise, so he gave Wang a drink of something delicious and cool, and went away.

When Little-Third-One had drunk this, his fever fell, and he was able to enjoy a little sleep. He was awakened by a slight noise. The night was come. The room was lighted by the full moon, which threw a bright gleam through the open door.

Then he saw that the room was full of insects that were moving and flying hither and thither. There were white ants that gnaw wood, bad-smelling bugs, enormous cockroaches, mosquitoes, and many many flies. And they were all buzzing, gnashing their teeth, or falling.

As Little-Third-One looked, he saw something move on the threshold. A small man, not bigger than a thumb, advanced with cautious steps. In his hand he held a bow; a sword was hanging by his side.

Little-Third-One, looking closer, saw two dogs as big as shirt-buttons, running in front of the little man. They suddenly stopped. The archer approached nearer to the bed, and held out his bow, and discharged a tiny arrow. A cockroach that was crawling before the dogs, made a bound, fell on its back, kicked, and was motionless. The arrow had run through it.

Behind the little man, other little men had come. Some rode on small horses, and were armed with swords, and still others were on foot. All these huntsmen scattered about the room, and ran or rode, to and fro, shooting arrows, and brandishing their swords; until hundreds and hundreds of insects were killed. At first the mosquitoes escaped, but, as they cannot fly for long, every time one of them settled on the wall, it was transfixed by a huntsman.

Soon none were left of all the insects that had broken the silence with their buzzing, their gnashing of teeth, and their falling.

A horseman then galloped around the room, looking from right to left. He gave a signal. All the huntsmen called their dogs, went to the door, and disappeared.

Little-Third-One had not moved, for fear that he should disturb the hunt. At last he went peacefully to sleep, and woke the next day cured. When his friend the Magician came to see him, Little-Third-One told him about the mysterious huntsmen, and his friend the Magician smiled.

HOW PEEPING KATE
WAS PISKEY-LED

From Cornwall

'T is Hallowe'en Night, Teddy, my boy. Don't go out on the moor, or near the Gump, for the Piskeys and the Spriggans are abroad, waiting to mislead straying mortals. Many are the men and women that the Little People have whisked away on Hallowe'en Night; and the poor mortals have never been heard of since.

Sit down, Teddy, my boy, crack these nuts, and eat these red apples; and I'll tell you how Peeping Kate was Piskey-led.

I have heard the old folks say how long ago—maybe a hundred years or so—the Squire of Pendeen had a housekeeper, an elderly dame, called Kate Tregeer.

Well, one Hallowe'en Night, some spices and other small things were wanted for the feasten-tide, and Kate would not trust any one to go for them except herself. So she put on her red coat and high steeple-crowned hat, and walked to Penzance. She bought the goods and started for home.

It was a bright moonlight night, and though no wind was blowing, the leaves of the trees were murmuring with a hollow sound. And Kate could hear strange rustlings in the bushes by the side of the road.

She had walked a very long time, and her basket was so heavy that she began to feel tired. Her legs bent under her and she could scarcely stand up. Just then she beheld, a little in front of her, a man on horseback. And she could tell by the proud way he sat that he was a gentleman-born.

She was very glad to see him, and as he was going slowly, she soon overtook him; and when she came up, his horse stood stock-still.

"My dear Master," she said, "how glad I am to see you. Don't you know me? I'm Kate Tregeer of Pendeen; and I can't tell you how hard I've worked all day."

Then she explained to him how she had walked to Penzance, and was now so tired that she could not stand up. But the gentleman made no reply.

"My dear Master," said she, "I'm footsore and leg-weary. I've got as far as here, you see, but I can get no farther. Do have pity on a poor unfortunate woman, and take her behind you. I can ride well enough on your horse's back without a saddle or pillion."

But still the gentleman made no reply.

"My dear Master," she said again, "My! but you're a fine-looking man! How upright you sit on your horse! But why don't you answer me? Are you asleep? One would think you were taking a nap; and your horse, too, it is standing so still!"

Not having any word in reply to this fine speech, Kate called out as loud as she could: "Even if you are a gentleman-born, you needn't be so stuck-up that you won't speak to a poor body afoot!"

Still he never spoke, though Kate thought that she saw him wink at her.

This vexed her the more. "The time was when the Tregeers were among the first in the parish, and were buried with the gentry! Wake up and speak to me!" screamed she in a rage. And then she took up a stone, and threw it at the horse. The stone rolled back to her feet, and the animal did not even whisk its tail.

Kate now got nearer, and saw that the rider had no hat on, nor was there any hair on his bald head. She touched the horse, and felt nothing but a bunch of furze. She rubbed her eyes and saw at once, to her great astonishment, that it was no gentleman and horse at all, only a smooth stone half buried in a heap of furze. And there she was still far away from Pendeen, with her heavy basket, and her legs so tired that she could scarcely move. And then she saw that she had come a short distance only, and knew that she must be bewitched.

Well, on she went; and seeing a light at her left hand she thought that it shone from the window of a house where she might rest awhile. So she made for it straight across the moor, floundering through bogs, and tripping over bunches of furze. And still the light was always just ahead, and it seemed to move from side to side. Then suddenly it went out, and she was left standing in a bog. The next minute she found herself among furze-ricks and pigsties, in the yard of Farmer Boslow, miles away from Pendeen.

She opened the door of an old outhouse, and entered, hoping to get a few hours' rest. There she lay down on straw and fell asleep; but she was soon wakened by some young pigs who were rooting around in the straw. That was too much for Kate. So up she got, and as she did so she heard the noise of a flail. And seeing a glimmer of light in a barn near by, she crept softly to a little window in the barn, and peeped to find what was going on.

At first she could see only two rush-wicks burning in two old iron lamps. Then through the dim light she saw the slash-flash of a flail as it rose and fell, and beat the barn floor. She stood on tiptoes, and stuck her head in farther, and whom did she see, wielding the flail, but a little old man, about three feet high, with hair like a bunch of rushes, and ragged clothes. His face was broader than it was long, and he had great owl-eyes shaded by heavy eyebrows from which his nose poked like a pig's snout. Kate noticed that his teeth were crooked and jagged, and that at each stroke of the flail, he kept moving his thin lips around and around, and thrusting his tongue in and out. His shoulders were broad enough for a man twice his height, and his feet were splayed like a frog's.

"Well! Well!" thought Kate. "This is luck! To see the Piskey threshing! For ever since I can remember I have heard it said that the Piskey threshed corn for Farmer Boslow on winter nights, and did other odd jobs for him the year round. But I would not believe it. Yet here he is!"

Then she reached her head farther in, and beheld a score of little men helping the Piskey. Some of them were lugging down the sheaves, and placing them handy for him; and others were carrying away the straw from which the grain had been threshed. Soon a heap of corn was gathered on the floor, as clean as if it had been winnowed.

In doing this the Piskey raised such a dust that it set him and some of the little men sneezing. And Kate, without stopping to think, called out:—

"God bless you, little men!"

Quick as a wink the lights vanished, and a handful of dust was thrown into her eyes, which blinded her so that for a moment she could not see. And then she heard the Piskey squeak:—

"I spy thy face,
Old Peeping Kate,
I'll serve thee out,
Early and late!"

Kate, when she heard this, felt very uneasy, for she remembered that the Little People have a great spite against any one who peeps at them, or pries into their doings.

The night being clear, she quickly found her way out of the crooked lane, and ran as fast as she could, and never stopped until she reached the Gump. There she sat down to rest awhile.

After that she stood up; and turn whichever way she might the same road lay before her. Then she knew that the Piskey was playing her a trick. So she ran down a hill as fast as she could, not caring in what direction she was going, so long as she could get away from the Piskey.

After running a long while, she heard music and saw lights at no great distance. Thinking that she must be near a house, she went over the downs toward the lights, feeling ready for a jig, and stopping now and then to dance around and around to the strains of the music.

But instead of arriving at a house, in passing around some high rocks she came out on a broad green meadow, encircled with furze and rocks. And there before her she saw a whole troop of Spriggans holding an Elfin Fair. It was like a feasten-day. Scores of little booths were standing in rows, and were covered with tiny trinkets such as buckles of silver and gold glistening with Cornish diamonds, pins with jewelled heads, brooches, rings, bracelets, and necklaces of crystal beads, green and red or blue and gold; and many other pretty things new to Kate.

There were lights in all directions—lanterns no bigger than Foxgloves were hanging in rows; and on the booths, rushlights in tulip-cups shone among Fairy goodies such as Kate had never dreamed of. Yet with all these lights there was such a shimmer over everything that she got bewildered, and could not see as plainly as she wished.

She did not care to disturb the Little People until she had looked at all that was doing. So she crept softly behind the booths and watched the Spriggans dancing. Hundreds of them, linked hand in hand, went whirling around so fast as to make her dizzy. Small as they were, they were all decked out like rich folk, the little men in cocked hats and feathers, blue coats gay with lace and gold buttons, breeches and stockings of lighter hue, and tiny shoes with diamond buckles.

Kate could not name the colours of the little ladies' dresses, which were of all the hues of Summer blossoms. The vain little things had powdered their hair, and decked their heads with ribbons, feathers, and flowers. Their shoes were of velvet and satin, and were high-heeled and pointed. And such sparkling black eyes as all the little ladies had, and such dimpled cheeks and chins! And they were merry, sprightly, and laughing.

All the Spriggans were capering and dancing around a pole wreathed with flowers. The pipers, standing in their midst, played such lively airs that Kate never in all her life had wanted to dance more. But she kept quite still, for she did not wish the Little People to know that she was there. She was determined to pocket some of the pretty things in the booths, and steal softly away with them. She thought how nice a bright pair of diamond buckles would look on her best shoes, and how fine her Sunday cap would be ornamented with a Fairy brooch.

So she raised her hand and laid it on some buckles, when— oh! oh!—she felt a palmful of pins and needles stick into her fingers like red-hot points; and she screamed:—

"Misfortune take you, you bad little Spriggans!"

Immediately the lights went out, and she felt hundreds of the Little People leap on her back, and her neck, and her head. At the same moment others tripped up her heels, and laid her flat on the ground, and rolled her over and over.

Then she caught sight of the Piskey mounted on a wild-looking colt, his toes stuck in its mane. He was holding a rush for a whip.

And there he sat grinning from ear to ear, and urging on the Spriggans to torment her, with "Haw! Haw! Haw!" and "Tee! Hee! Hee!"

She spread out her arms and squeezed herself tight to the ground, so that the Spriggans might not turn her over; but they squeaked and grunted, and over and over she went. And every time that they turned her face downward, some of the little fellows jumped on her back, and jigged away from her toe to her head.

She reached around to beat them off with a stick, but they pulled it out of her hand; and, balancing it across her body, strided it, and bobbed up and down, singing:—

> "See-saw-pate!
> Lie still old Peeping Kate!
> See-saw-pate!
> Here we'll ride, early and late,
> On the back of Peeping Kate!"

And with that, poor Kate, not to be beaten by the Spriggans, tossed back her feet to kick the little fellows away, but they pulled off her shoes and tickled and prickled the soles of her feet until she fell a-laughing and a-crying by turns.

Kate was almost mad with their torment, when by good chance she remembered a charm that she would drive away all mischievous spirits, on Hallowe'en. So she repeated it forwards and backwards, and in a twinkling all the little Spriggans fled screeching away, the Piskey galloping after them.

Then she got on her feet and looked around. She saw, by the starlight of a clear frosty morning, that the place to which she had been Piskey-led was a green spot near the Gump, where folks said the Spriggans held their nightly revels. And although the spot was very small, it had seemed to her like a ten-acre field because of enchantment.

And her hat, and her shoes, and her basket were gone; and poor Kate, barefooted and bare-headed, had to hobble home as best she could. And she reached Pendeen gate more dead than alive.

ONE-EYED PRYING JOAN'S TALE

From Cornwall

Sit down, Bobby, my boy. Eat some bread and cheese. Don't be afraid to drink the cider. It's all my own making. Sit down, and I'll tell you how I lost the sight of my right eye.

The last Christmas Eve I went to Penzance to buy a pair of shoes for myself, and some thread and buttons, and things to mend Master's clothes. I dearly like company, and as I started out I thought of old Betty down at the cove, she that they say is a Witch, you know.

Thinks I to myself: "If she's a Witch, she'll not hurt me, as I never crossed her in my life. Witch or no Witch, I'll stop and have a bite of something hot at her little house," thought I.

When I came to the house, the door was tight shut, and I heard a strange mumbling inside, but I could not make out what it was. So I took a peep through the latch-hole. And what did I see but old Betty standing by the chimney-piece with a little box in her hand, and she was muttering something that sounded like a charm. She put her finger into the box and pulled it out again, and smeared some ointment over her eyes. Then she put the box into a hole near the chimney.

I lifted the latch and walked in. "How-de-do, Betty," said I.

"Welcome," said she, grinning and pleased. "Sit down by the fire. Now we'll have a good drop of something hot to ourselves, seeing that it's Christmas Eve," said she.

"I'll take a thimbleful, just to drink your health and a Merry Christmas to you, with all my heart," said I; for I well knew that Betty made the best sweet drink, with sugar and spice and a roasted apple bobbing around in it.

I put down my basket, and took off my coat, and sat by the fire; while Betty stepped into a closet to fetch the cups.

Now, I had often wondered what made her eyes so clear and piercing. "'Tis the Fairy ointment, or Witch salve in the box," thought I. "If it will do that to her eyes, it won't hurt me." So while she was gone, I took the box from the hole, where she had covered it with ferns, and put a bit of the ointment on my right eye. The stuff had no sooner touched me than it burned like fire, or as if needles and pins were being thrust into my eyeball. Just then Betty came from the closet, and I dragged the brim of my hat down over my right eye, so she should not see what had happened.

After we had drunk each other's health three or four times, the pain went off, and I ventured to open my anointed eye. And oh! what did I see! The place was full of Spriggans! Troops of the Little People were cutting all sorts of capers in the folds of the nets and sails hung on the walls, in the bunches of herbs that swung from the rafters, and in the pots and pans on the dresser. Some of them were playing seesaw on the beams of the ceiling, tossing their heels and waving their feathered caps, as they teetered up and down on bits of straw or green twigs. Numbers of them were swinging in the cobwebs that festooned the rafters or riding mice in and out through holes in the thatch.

I noted that all the little men were dressed in green tricked out with red, and had feathered caps and high riding-boots with silver spurs. Their ladies, if you please, were all decked in grand fashion—their gowns were of green velvet with long trains and looped up with silver chains and bells. They wore high-crowned steeple-hats, with wreaths of the most beautiful flowers around them; while sprigs of blossoms and garlands decorated all parts of their dress, and were in their hands as well. They were the sauciest Little People I ever did see. They pranced around on their high-heeled boots sparkling with diamond buckles.

When I peeped into the wood-corner under Betty's bunk, I spied some of the ugly Spriggans sitting there looking very gloomy because they have to watch the treasures that are hidden in the ground, and do other disagreeable things that the merry Spriggans never have to do.

While looking into the dark corner I heard strains of sweet, unearthly music outside the house. Glancing around the room, I saw that all was changed. The walls were hung with tapestry, the chimney stools on which we sat were carved chairs. Betty and I sat under a canopy of embroidered satin, and our feet rested on a silken carpet. And wherever the little Spriggans trod, they left circles like diamonds on the floor.

The sweet music was now close at hand under the little window, and a moment after a troop of the Little People appeared on the window-sill, playing on pipes, flutes, and other instruments made of green reeds from the brook and of shells from the shore.

The Fairy band stepped down most gracefully from the window-sill, and was closely followed by a long train of little men and women magnificently dressed, and carrying bunches of flowers in their hands. All walked in an orderly procession, two by two, and bowed or curtsied, to Betty, and cast the flowers in her lap. I saw their many bunches of Four-leaved Clover and sprigs of magic herbs. With these she makes her salves and lotions.

Then all the Spriggans who had been dancing and capering about the ceiling and floor joined the others and came crowding around Betty. She did not look surprised, and I did not say anything to let her know that I saw. The Spriggans then began to pour dew over her dress out of flower-buds and from the bottles of the Foxglove. Immediately her jacket was changed into the finest and richest cloth of a soft cream colour, and her dress became velvet the colour of all the flowers, and it was draped over a petticoat of silk quilted with silver cord.

The Little People brought tiny nosegays of sky-blue Pimpernel, Forget-me-nots, and dainty flower-bells, blue, pink, and white, and hundreds of other Fairy blossoms like stars and butterflies. These delicate little sprigs they stitched all over Betty's silver-corded petticoat together with branching moss and the lace-like tips of the wild grass. All around the bottom of her skirt they made a wreath of tiny bramble leaves with roses and berries, red and black.

Many of the Little People perched themselves on the top of the high-backed chair in which Betty sat, and even stood on her shoulders, so that they might arrange her every curl and every hair. Some took the lids off pretty little urns they carried in their hands, and poured perfume on her head, which spread the sweetest odours through the room. I very much admired the lovely little urns, with their grooved lids, but when I picked one up, it was only a seed-pod of the wild Poppy. They placed no other ornament in her hair except a small twig of holly full of bright red berries. Yet Betty, decked out by her Fairy friends, was more beautiful than the loveliest Queen of May.

My senses were overcome by the smell of the Fairy odours, and the scent of the flowers, and the sweet perfume of honey, with which the walls of the house seemed bursting. And my head fell forward and I slept.

How long I dozed I do not know, but when I woke I saw that all the little Spriggans were glaring at me angrily. They thrust out their tongues and made the most horrid grimaces. I was so frightened that I jumped up, and ran out of the house, and shut the door.

But for the life of me, I could not leave the place without taking another peep. I put my left eye to the latch-hole—and would you believe it?—the house was just as it was when I entered it; the floor was bare, and there sat Betty in her old clothes before the fire. Then I winked, and looked with the right eye, and there was the beautiful room, and Betty seated in her fine flower-gown, beneath the silken canopy, while all the little Spriggans were dancing and capering around her.

I tore myself away, glad to get out of the cove, and hurried to Penzance to do my shopping, although it was so late. And as I was standing in front of a booth, what should I see but a little Spriggan helping himself to hanks of yarn, stockings, and all sorts of fine things.

"Ah! Ha! my little man!" cried I. "Are you not ashamed to be carrying on this way, stealing all those goods?"

"Is that thee, old Joan?" said he. "Which eye canst thou see me with?"

After winking both my eyes, I said: "'Tis plain enough that I can see you with my right eye."

Then in a twinkling he pointed his finger at my right eye, and mumbled a spell, and I just caught the words:—

"Joan the Pry
Shall nor peep nor spy,
But shall lose
Her charmèd eye!"

Then he blew in my face, and was gone. And when I looked around, my right eye was blind. And from that day to this I have never seen a blink with my anointed eye.

VI. *Fairy Servants in the House*

THE FAIRY'S SERVANTS

From the Basque

O nce upon a time there was a poor woman who had three
daughters.

One day the youngest said: "Mother, now that I am old
enough, I wish to go out to service."

The mother thought to herself: "If this one goes, why, there
will be more to eat for the rest of us," so she said: "Very well,
good luck go with you."

The girl set out, and after she had walked a long way she came
to a beautiful city. A handsome lady met her, and asked:—

"Where are you going, my child?"

"I am going out to service," replied the girl.

"Will you come with me to my home?" asked the lady.

"Yes, indeed," said the girl, "and I'll try to serve you faithfully."

The lady led her to a large and fine house, and told her what
work she should do that day.

"We are Fairies," said she. "I must go away for a short time,
but do your work in the kitchen while I am gone. Dig up the
kitchen floor, smash the pitcher, break the plates. Whip the children, throw dirt in their faces, and rumple their hair." Then the
lady went away.

The girl, who thought these orders very strange, began to
feed the children. Just then a little dog came creeping up to her,
wagging his tail.

"Bow! Bow! Bow!" said he. "I, too, want something to eat!"

So the girl gave him a plateful of breakfast, and when he had
eaten all he wished, he said:—

"You are a good girl, and I will tell you what to do to please
my mistress. What she really meant was for you to sweep the
kitchen floor, fill the pitcher, wash the dishes, and dress and

feed the children. Do all this well, and she will give you the choice of a beautiful star on your forehead or a donkey's tail hanging from your nose. Then she will offer you a sack of gold or a bag of charcoal. You must choose the donkey's tail and the bag of charcoal."

Well, the girl did all as the little dog told her, and when the mistress came home she smiled and said:—

"Choose which you will have, a beautiful star on your forehead, or a donkey's tail hanging from your nose."

"A donkey's tail is the same to me," said the girl.

"Will you have a sack of gold or a bag of charcoal?" asked the lady.

"The bag of charcoal is the same to me," said the girl.

Then the lady placed a beautiful star on her forehead, and gave her a big sackful of gold, and told her she might go back to her mother.

The girl thanked the lady, and leaving the house hastened home. When her mother and sisters saw how pretty she was with the star on her forehead, and when they felt the big sack of gold on her shoulder, they were astonished.

Then the eldest sister began to cry and say: "Mother, I will go out and be a servant, too!"

"No! no! my child," said the mother, "I will not let you go."

But the girl wept, and would not leave her mother in peace until she said, "Go"; then she set off and walked until she came to the Fairy city.

The handsome lady met her and asked:—

"Where are you going, my child?"

"I am going out to service," said the girl.

"Will you come with me to my home?" asked the lady.

The girl said she would, so the lady led her to the large and fine house and told her what work she should do that day.

"Dig up the kitchen floor," said she, "smash the pitcher, break the plates. Whip the children, throw dirt in their faces, and rumple their hair." Then she went away.

As soon as the lady was gone, the girl began to eat up all the good things in the pantry. Just then the little dog came creeping up to her, wagging his tail.

"Bow! Bow! Bow! I, too, want something to eat," he said.

"Go away, you horrid little beast," answered the girl, and she gave him a kick.

But the dog would not leave her, and followed her about until she drove him from the kitchen with blows. Then she dug up the kitchen floor, smashed the pitcher, broke all the plates, whipped the children, threw dirt in their faces, and rumpled their hair.

By and by the mistress came home, and when she saw what the girl had been doing she frowned and said:—

"Choose which you will have, a beautiful star on your forehead or a donkey's tail hanging from your nose."

"A star on my forehead for me," said the girl.

"Will you have a sack of gold or a bag of charcoal?" asked the lady.

"A sack of gold for me," said the girl.

Then the lady hung a donkey's tail on the end of her nose, and gave her a big bag of charcoal, and sent her back to her home. And when her mother saw her she was so ashamed that she locked her in the cellar.

As for the youngest girl, she shared her sack of gold with her mother and other sister, and then she married a fine young man, and lived happily ever after.

THE PIXIES

From England

There was once a little cottage in the middle of a flower garden. Its walls were covered with roses, and its porch was
twined with clematis. The bees buzzed over the flowers, and the
butterflies fluttered about the porch. And a hundred little green
Pixies lived in the wood near by.

In this cottage two orphan sisters dwelt all alone. One morning the elder sister, Mary, got up at break of day. She milked the
cow, churned the butter, swept the hearth, and made the breakfast. Then she sat on the porch to spin, and sang:—

> *"How merrily the wheel goes round,*
> *With a whirring, humming sound!"*

But the youngest sister, Alice, lay in bed asleep. Then Mary
put her spinning aside, and called:—

"Wake, Alice, wake! There is much for you to do while I go to
the market-town. I must sell our yarn, and buy your new dress.
While I am gone, don't forget to bring in the firewood, drain the
honeycomb, and fill the Pixies' water-pail."

But Alice did not answer. So Mary put on her hood and took
her basket full of yarn. She walked all the way to the market-
town and sold her yarn, and bought the new dress. Then she
walked home again.

The sun was set when she reached the cottage, and Alice was
sitting idle on the porch. The honeycomb was not drained, the
firewood was not brought in, the bed was not made, and the
supper was uncooked. And although Mary was tired and hungry,
she had to cook the supper and make the bed. Then the sisters
went to sleep.

By and by, the hundred little green Pixies came creeping, creeping into the kitchen. They pattered softly about and whispered

so that the sisters should not hear them. Some ran to the spinning-wheel and began to spin, others built a fire under the oven, and mixed and kneaded the bread. One took a broom and swept the floor, and another brought in the firewood.

When all the yarn was spun, the bread baked, and the kitchen tidy, the Pixies ran to the water-pail to get a drink. But there was not a drop of water in it! And, oh! how angry they were!

Then Mary awoke, and cried: "Alice! Alice! Don't you hear those angry buzzings? Surely you did not forget to fill the Pixies' water-pail!"

But Alice answered: "I did not draw the water to-day. And I will not leave my bed now to fetch it for any little Pixy!" Then she went to sleep again.

But Mary got up, and, though her feet were tired and sore, she took the pail and ran through the garden to the spring. And as she stooped she saw a hundred little faces laughing at her from the water. She dipped her pail, and they were gone. She lifted the full pail, and felt little hands seize it and bear it along. It was carried to the door, and into the kitchen, and set down by the hearth. But she could see no one, so she went to bed again.

The next morning early, Mary got up. She ran to the pail and looked into it. Then she clapped her hands and called:—

"Come, Alice, come! See the silver pennies shining at the bottom of the clear water! There must be a hundred of them! Come, sister, dear!"

Then Alice, waking, tried to sit up. But she screamed with fright, for she could not move her hands and feet. Indeed, she could not rise at all! And that day, and the next, and for many days after, she lay helpless on her bed, and Mary fed and comforted her.

And every night the hundred little green Pixies came creeping, creeping into the kitchen. They swept, they baked, they sewed, they spun, and they drank from Mary's water-pail. And every night they left one piece of silver there.

And so a whole year passed, and Alice lay and thought, and thought, and thought about her idle ways. And one night she called Mary to her, and wept and said:—

"Oh, sister, if only I could get up to-morrow, and feel the

warm sunshine and play among the flowers! And if only I were strong enough to work for you, as you have worked for me!"

And Mary kissed and comforted her.

The next morning came, and Mary got up at break of day. She ran and looked into the water-pail. Then she clapped her hands and called:—

"Come, Alice, come! See the silver pennies shining at the bottom of the clear water! There must be a hundred of them! Come, sister, dear!"

And Alice forgot that she could not move. She sprang lightly out of bed and ran into the kitchen. And she was all well and happy again!

And oh, how glad the sisters were! How they kissed each other and laughed with joy! They milked the cow, and churned, and baked, and cooked, and sat spinning on the porch. And the bees buzzed, and the butterflies fluttered, and the sisters sang:—

> *"How merrily the wheels go round,*
> *With a whirring, humming sound!"*

THE BROWNIE OF BLEDNOCH

From Scotland

OLD MADGE'S TALE

Have you ever heard of the Brownie, Aiken-Drum? No? Well, I will tell you how he came to Blednoch. It was in the Autumn time. The red sun was setting, when through our town he passed crying, oh! so wearily:—

> *"Have ye work for Aiken-Drum?*
> *Have ye work for Aiken-Drum?"*

He tirled at the pin, and entered in. I trow the boldest there stood back! You should have heard the children scream. The black dog barked, the lasses shrieked, at the sight of Aiken-Drum.

His matted head lay on his breast. A long blue beard fell to his waist. Around his hairy form was wrapped a cloth of woven rushes green. His long, thin arms trailed on the ground. His hands were claws; his feet had no toes. Oh, fearful to see was Aiken-Drum! And all the time he cried so wearily, so drearily:—

> *"Have ye work for Aiken-Drum?*
> *Have ye work for Aiken-Drum?"*

Then the brave goodman stood forth, and said: "What would you? Whence come you by land or sea?"

Then what a groan gave Aiken-Drum! "I come from a land where I never saw the sky! But now I'll bide with you, if ye have work for Aiken-Drum! I'll watch your sheep and tend your kine, each night till day. I'll thresh your grain by the light of the moon. I'll sing strange songs to your bonny bairns, if ye'll but keep poor Aiken-Drum! I'll churn the cream, I'll knead the bread, I'll tame the wildest colts ye have, if ye'll but keep poor Aiken-Drum! No

76

clothes nor gold is wage for me. A bowl of porridge on the warm hearthstone is wage enough for Aiken-Drum!"

"The Brownie speaks well," said the old housewife. "Our workers are scarce. We have much to do. Let us try this Aiken-Drum."

Then should you have seen the Brownie work! By night he swept the kitchen clean. He scoured the pots until they shone. By the light of the moon he threshed the grain. He gathered the crops into the barn. He watched the sheep and tended the kine. By day he played with the bonny bairns, and sang them strange songs of the land without sky. So passed the months away, and all farm-things throve for the goodman and the old housewife.

But when the cold night winds blew hard, a lass, who saw the Brownie's clothes woven all of rushes green, made him a suit of sheep's wool warm. She placed it by his porridge bowl. And that night was heard a wailing cry, so weary and so dreary:—

> *"Long, long may I now weep and groan!*
> *Wages of clothes are now my own!*
> *O luckless Aiken-Drum!"*

And down the street and through the town, his voice came back upon the wind:—

> *"Farewell to Blednoch!*
> *Farewell! Farewell!"*

And never again in all that land was seen the Brownie Aiken-Drum!

ELSA AND THE TEN ELVES

From Sweden

O nce upon a time a little girl named Elsa lived on a farm. She was pretty, sweet-tempered, and generous, but she did not like to work. Her father was very proud of her, and sent her to school in the city. She learned to read, write, sing, and dance, but still she did not know how to cook, sew, or care for a house.

When she grew older, she was so good and beautiful that many young men wished her for a wife, but she said "No" to all except to her neighbour, Gunner, a handsome, industrious young farmer. Soon they were married, and went to live on his farm.

At first all was happiness, but as the days passed, and Elsa did not direct the servants or look after the house, everything went wrong. The storerooms were in disorder, the food was stolen, and the house dirty. Poor Gunner was at his wits' end; he loved Elsa too much to scold her.

The day before Christmas came, the sun had been up for a long time, and still Elsa lay in bed. A servant ran into her room, saying:—

"Dear mistress, shall we get ready the men's luncheon so that they may go to the woods?"

"Leave the room," said Elsa sleepily, "and do not waken me again!"

Another servant came running in. "Dear mistress," she cried, "the leaven is working, and if you come quickly the bread will be better than usual."

"I want candlewicks, dear mistress," called a third.

"And what meat shall we roast for to-morrow's feast?" shouted a fourth.

And so it was; servant after servant came running into the room asking for orders, but Elsa would neither answer nor get up.

Last of all came Gunner, impatient because his men had not yet started for the woods.

"Dear Elsa," he said gently, "my mother used to prepare things the night before, so that the servants might begin work early. We are now going to the woods, and shall not be back until night. Remember there are a few yards of cloth on the loom waiting to be woven." Then Gunner went away.

As soon as he was gone, Elsa got up in a rage, and, dressing herself, ran through the kitchen to the little house where the loom was kept. She slammed the door behind her, and threw herself down on a couch.

"No!" she screamed. "I won't!—I won't endure this drudgery any more! Who would have thought that Gunner would make a servant of me, and wear my life out with work? Oh, me! Oh, me! Is there no one from far or near to help me?"

"I can," said a deep voice.

And Elsa, raising her head with fright, saw standing close to her an old man wrapped in a gray cloak and wearing a broad-brimmed hat.

"I am Old Man Hoberg," he said, "and have served your family for many generations. You, my child, are unhappy because you are idle. To love work is a joy. I will now give you ten obedient servants who shall do all your tasks for you."

He shook his cloak, and out of its folds tumbled ten funny little men. They capered and pranced about, making faces. Then they swiftly put the room in order and finished weaving the cloth on the loom. After all was done they ran and stood in an obedient row before Elsa.

"Dear child, reach hither your hands," said the old man.

And Elsa, trembling, gave him the tips of her fingers.

Then he said:—

> "Hop-o'-My-Thumb,
> Lick-the-Pot,
> Long-Pole,
> Heart-in-Hand,
> Little-Peter-Funny-Man,
> Away all of you to your places!"

And in the twinkling of an eye the little men vanished into Elsa's fingers, and the old man disappeared.

Elsa could hardly believe what had happened, and sat staring at her hands. Suddenly a wonderful desire to work came over her. She could sit still no longer.

"Why am I idling here?" cried she cheerfully. "It is late in the morning and the house is not in order! The servants are waiting." And up she jumped and hastened into the kitchen, and was soon giving orders and singing while she prepared the dinner.

And when Gunner came home that night all was clean and bright to welcome him, and the smell of good things to eat filled the house.

And after that day Elsa rose early each morning, and went about her work sweet-tempered and happy. No one was more pleased and proud than she to see how the work of the farm-house prospered under her hands. And health, wealth, and happiness came and stayed with Elsa and Gunner.

PISKEY FINE! AND PISKEY GAY!

From Cornwall

'Tis told in the west country, how the Piskey threshed the corn, and did other odd jobs for Farmer Boslow as long as the old man lived. And after his death the Piskey worked for his widow. And this is how she lost the little fellow.

One night, when the hills were covered with snow, and the wind was blowing hard, the Widow Boslow left in the barn, for the Piskey, a larger bowl than usual full of milk thickened with oatmeal. It was clear moonlight, and she stopped outside the door, and peeped in to see if the Piskey would come to eat his supper while it was hot.

The moonlight shone through a little window on to the barn floor; and there, sitting on a sheaf of oats, she saw the Piskey greedily eating his thickened milk. He soon emptied the bowl and scraped it as clean with the wooden spoon as if it had been washed. Then he placed them both in a corner, and stood up and patted and stroked his stomach, and smacked his lips, as if to say: "That's good of the old dear! See if I don't thresh well for her to-night!"

But when the Piskey turned around, the widow saw that he had nothing on but rags, and very few of them.

"How the poor Piskey must suffer!" thought she. "He has to pass most of his time out among the rushes in the boggy moor, and his legs are naked, and his breeches are full of holes. I'll make the poor fellow a good warm suit of homespun, at once!"

No sooner thought than she went home and began the suit. In a day or two she had made a coat and breeches, and knitted a long pair of sheep's wool stockings, with garters and a nightcap all nicely knitted, too.

When night came, the widow placed the Piskey's new clothes and a big bowl of thickened milk on the barn floor, just where the moonlight fell brightest. Then she went outside, and peeped through the door.

Soon she saw the Piskey eating his supper, and squinting at the new clothes. Laying down his empty bowl, he took the things, and put them on over his rags. Then he began capering and jumping around the barn, singing:—

> *"Piskey fine! and Piskey gay!*
> *Piskey now will run away!"*

And sure enough, he bolted out of the door, and passed the widow, without so much as "I wish you well till I see you again!" And he never came back to the farm.

THE FAIRY WEDDING

From Sweden

Once upon a time there was a lovely young girl, daughter of rich parents, who was known for her gentleness and goodness.

One night, while she was lying awake in her bed, watching the moonbeams dance on the floor, her door was softly opened. Then in tripped a little Fairy man clad in a gray jacket and red cap. He came lightly toward her bed, nodding in a most friendly way.

"Do not be afraid, dear lady," he said. "I have come to ask a favour of you."

"And I will do it willingly, if I can," answered the girl, who had begun to recover from her fright.

"Oh, it will not be difficult!" said the Fairy man. "For many years I and mine have lived under the floor of your kitchen, just where the water-cask stands. But the cask has become old and leaky, so that we are continually annoyed by the dripping of water. Our home is never dry."

"That shall be seen to in the morning," said the girl.

"Thank you, dear lady," said the Fairy man, and making an elegant bow, he disappeared as softly as he had come.

The next day, at the girl's request, her parents had the water-cask removed. And after that, to the surprise of the servants, the kitchen-work was done at night when all slept, and never a pitcher or glass was broken in the house from that day forth. So the Fairies showed their gratitude.

Well, a few months after this, the pretty young girl was again lying awake in her bed, watching the moonbeams dance on the floor, when again her door was opened softly, and the Fairy man stole in.

"Dear lady," said he, smiling and bowing, "now I have another request to make, which, in your kindness, you will surely not refuse to grant."

"What is it?" asked she.

"Will you honour me and my house, to-night," he replied, "and stand at the christening of my newly born daughter?"

The girl arose and dressing herself, followed the Fairy man through many passages and rooms that she had never known existed. At last they entered a small but elegant apartment, in which a host of Fairies were assembled. They immediately christened the Fairy baby. And as the little man was about to conduct the girl again to her room, the Fairies filled her pockets with what looked like shavings.

The little man then led her back through the same winding passages, and as soon as she was safely in her room, he said:—

"If we should meet at another time, you must never laugh at me and mine. We love you for your goodness and modesty, but if you laugh at us, you and I shall never see each other again."

When he was gone the girl threw all the shavings into the fireplace, and lay down, and went to sleep. And, lo, the next morning when the maid came in to build the fire, she found in the ashes the most beautiful jewelry, all of pure gold set with gems, and of the finest workmanship!

Now, it happened, some time after this, that the girl's wedding day arrived. There was great bustling, and preparations for a splendid feast. At length the wedding hour came. The bride, beautifully dressed and wearing her Fairy jewels and a crown on her golden hair, was conducted to the hall where the guests were waiting.

During the ceremony she chanced to glance around the hall. She saw, near the fireplace, all her friends the Fairies gathered for a wedding feast. The bridegroom was a little Elf, and the bride was her goddaughter, and the feast was spread on a golden table.

No one but the girl could see the Fairies. Just at that moment one of the Elves, who was acting as waiter at the Fairy bridal, stumbled over a twig that lay on the floor, and fell. Forgetting the caution that the little man had given her, the girl burst into a hearty laugh.

Instantly the golden table, the Elfin bridegroom and bride, and all the Fairy guests vanished. And from that day to this, no work was ever done at night in that kitchen, nor were any Fairies ever seen about that house.

THE TOMTS

From Sweden

E very child knows—or ought to know if he does not know—
that the Tomt is a queer little Elfin man, old and wizen, and
clad in gray clothes and red cap. He lives in the pantry or in the
barn. At night he washes the dishes and sweeps the kitchen
floor, or threshes the farmer's corn and looks after his sheep.
Oh, the Tomt is a very friendly Elf, but his feelings are easily
hurt! And if any one is impolite to him, he runs away, and is
never seen again.

Now, it happened, once upon a time, that there was a farmer
whose crops and flocks and herds prospered so well that all
knew he was aided by a Tomt. In fact he became the richest
farmer in his neighbourhood. Although he had few servants, his
house was always in order, and his grain nicely threshed. But he
never saw the Elf who did all these things for him.

One night he decided to watch and see who worked in his
barn. He hid behind a door. By and by he saw, not *one* Tomt, but
a *multitude* of Tomts come into the barn. Each carried a stalk of
rye; but the littlest Tomt of all, not bigger than a thumb, puffed
and breathed very hard, although he carried but a straw on his
shoulder.

"Why do you puff so hard?" cried the farmer from his hiding-
place. "Your burden is not so great!"

"His burden is according to his strength, for he is but one
night old," answered one of the Tomts. "Hereafter you shall
have less!"

And with that all the little men vanished, and the grain lay
unthreshed on the barn floor.

And from that day all luck disappeared from the farmer's
house, and he was soon reduced to beggary.

VII. Fays of Water, Wood, and Meadow

KINTARO THE GOLDEN BOY

From Japan

Once upon a time a poor widow and her little boy lived in a cave in the midst of a great forest. The little one's name was Kintaro the Golden Boy. He was a sturdy fellow with red cheeks and laughing eyes. He was different from other boys. When he fell down, he sang cheerily; if he wandered away from the cave, he could always find his way home again; and while he was yet very small, he could swing a heavy axe in circles round his head.

Kintaro grew to be ten years old, and a handsome, manly lad he was. Then his mother looked at him often and sighed deeply. "Must my child grow up in this lonely forest!" thought she sadly. "Will he never take his place in the world of men! Alas! Alas!"

But Kintaro was perfectly happy. The forest was full of his playmates. Every living thing loved him. When he lay on his bed of ferns, the birds flew nestling to his shoulder, and peeped into his eyes. The butterflies and moths settled on his face, and trod softly over his brown body. But his truest friends were the bears that dwelt in the forest. When he was tired of walking, a mother-bear carried him on her back. Her cubs ran to greet him, and romped and wrestled with him. Sometimes Kintaro would climb up the smooth-barked monkey-tree, and sit on the top-most bough, and laugh at the vain efforts of his shaggy cub-friends to follow him. Then came the bears' supper-time, and the feast of golden liquid honey!

Now it happened, one Summer, that there was to be a great day of sports for the forest creatures. Soon after dawn, a gentle-eyed stag came to waken Kintaro. The boy, with a farewell kiss to his mother, and a caress to the stag, leaped on his friend's back, and wound his arms around his soft neck. And away they went with long, noiseless bounds through the forest.

Up hill, across valleys, through thickets they bounded, until they reached a leafy spot in a wide, green glade near a foaming cataract. There the stag set Kintaro down; and the boy seated himself on a mossy stone, and began to whistle sweetly.

Immediately the forest rustled with living things. The song-birds came swiftly to his call. The eagle and the hawk flew from distant heights. The crane and the heron stepped proudly from their hyacinth-pools and hastened to the glade. All Kintaro's feathered friends flocked thither and rested in the cedar branches. Then through the undergrowth came running the wolf, the bear, the badger, the fox, and the martin, and seated themselves around Kintaro.

They all began to speak to him. He listened as they told their joys and sorrows, and he spoke graciously to each. For Kintaro had learned the languages of beasts, birds, and flowers.

And who had taught Kintaro all this? The Tengus, the Wood-Elves. And even while he was listening to the forest creatures, the Tengus themselves came tumbling out of the trees, or popping up from behind stones. Very strange little Elves they were! Each had the body of a man, the head of a hawk, powerful claws, and a long, long nose that usually trailed on the ground. And every little Tengu wore on his feet tiny stilt-like clogs.

All these queer Wood-Elves came toward Kintaro, walking very proudly with their arms crossed, heads well thrown back, and long noses held erect in the air. At their head was the Chief Tengu, very old, with a gray beard and a sharp beak.

The Chief Tengu seated himself beside Kintaro on the mossy stone, and waved a seven-feathered fan in the air. Immediately the sports began.

The young Tengus were fond of games. They found their long noses most useful. They now fenced with them, and balanced bowls full of gold-fish on them. Then two of the Tengus straightened their noses, and joined them together, and so made a tight rope. On this a young Tengu, with a paper umbrella in one hand, and leading a little dog with the other, danced and jumped through a hoop. And all the time an old Tengu sang a dance-song, and another Tengu beat time with a fan.

Kintaro cheered loudly, and clapped his hands; and the beasts and birds barked, hissed, growled, or sang for pleasure. So the morning passed swiftly and delightfully, and the time came for the forest animals to take part in the sports. They did so running, leaping, tumbling, and flying.

Last of all stood up a great father-bear to wrestle with Kintaro. Now, the boy had been taught to fight by his friends the Tengus; and he had learned from them many skilful tricks. So he and the bear gripped each other, and began to wrestle very hard. The bear was powerful and strong, and his claws like iron, but Kintaro was not afraid. Backward and forward they swayed, and struggled, while the Tengus and the forest creatures sat watching.

Now, it happened that the great Hero Raiko was just returning from slaying many horrible ogres and hags. His way lay through the forest, and at that moment he heard the noise of the wrestling. He stopped his horse and peered through the trees into the glade. There he saw the circle of animals and little Tengus, and Kintaro struggling with the powerful bear. Just at that moment the boy, with a skilful movement, threw the clumsy creature to the ground.

"I must have that boy for my son," thought Raiko. "He will make a great hero! He must be mine!"

So he waited until Kintaro had mounted the stag and bounded away through the forest. Then Raiko followed him on his swift steed to the cave.

When Kintaro's mother learned that Raiko was the mighty warrior who had slain the ogres and hags, she let him take her son to his castle. But before Kintaro went, he called together all his friends, the Tengus, the birds, and the beasts, and bade them farewell, in words that they remember to this day.

His mother did not follow her son to the land of men, for she loved the forest best; but Kintaro, when he became a great hero, often came to see her in her home. And all the people of Japan called him "Kintaro the Golden Boy."

THE FLOWER FAIRIES

From China

Once upon a time, high on a mountain-side, there was a place where many beautiful flowers grew, mostly Peonies and Camellias. A young man named Hwang, who wished to study all alone, built himself a little house near by.

One day he noticed from his window a lovely young girl dressed in white, wandering about among the flowers. He hastened out of the house to see who she was, but she ran behind a tall white Peony, and vanished.

Hwang was very much astonished, and sat down to watch. Soon the girl slipped from behind the white Peony, bringing another girl with her who was dressed in red. They wandered about hand in hand until they came near Hwang, when the girl in red gave a scream, and together the two ran back among the flowers, their robes and long sleeves fluttering in the wind and scenting all the air. Hwang dashed after them, but they had vanished completely.

That evening, as Hwang was sitting over his books, he was astonished to see the white girl walk into his little room. With tears in her eyes she seemed to be pleading with him to help her. Hwang tried to comfort her, but she did not speak. Then, sobbing bitterly, she suddenly vanished.

This appeared to Hwang as very strange. However, the next day a visitor came to the mountain, who, after wandering among the flowers, dug up the tall white Peony, and carried it off. Hwang then knew that the white girl was a Flower Fairy; and he became very sad because he had permitted the Peony to be carried away. Later he heard that the flower had lived only a few days. At this he wept, and, going to the place where the Peony had stood, watered the spot with his tears.

While he was weeping, the girl in red suddenly stood before him, wringing her hands, and wiping her eyes.

"Alas!" cried she, "that my dear sister should have been torn from my side! But the tears, Hwang, that you have shed, may be the means of restoring her to us!"

Having said this, the red girl disappeared. But that very night Hwang dreamed that she came to him, and seemed to implore him to help her, just as the white girl had done. In the morning he found that a new house was to be erected close by, and that the builder had given orders to cut down a beautiful tall red Camellia.

Hwang prevented the destruction of the flower; and that same evening, as he sat watching the Camellia, from behind its tall stem came the white girl herself, hand in hand with her red sister.

"Hwang," said the young girl, "the King of the Flower Fairies, touched by your tears, has restored my white sister to us. But as she is now only the ghost of a flower, she must dwell forever in a white Peony, and you will never see her again."

At these words Hwang caught hold of the white girl's hand, but it melted away in his; and both the sisters vanished forever from his sight. In despair he looked wildly around him, and all that he saw was a tall white Peony and a beautiful red Camellia.

After that Hwang pined, and fell ill, and died. He was buried at his own request, by the side of the white Peony; and before very long another white Peony grew up very straight and tall on Hwang's grave; so that the two flowers stood lovingly side by side.

THE FAIRY ISLAND

From Cornwall

In ancient days, in the land of Wales, there was a blue lake on a high mountain. No one had ever seen a bird fly near it. And over its waves came faint strains of delicious music, that seemed to float from a dimly seen island in its centre. No one had ever ventured to sail on its water, for every one knew that it was the abode of the Tylwyth Teg, the Water Fairies.

It happened, one lovely Summer day, that a hunter was wandering along the margin of the lake, and found himself before an open door in a rock. He entered, and walked along a dark passage that led downward. He followed this for some time, and suddenly found himself passing through another door, that opened on the mysterious, lovely island, the home of the Tylwyth Teg.

All around him was a most enchanting garden, where grew every sort of delicious fruit and fragrant flower. The next moment a number of Fairies advanced toward him, and graciously welcomed him to their abode. They bade him eat as much fruit as he wished, and pick the flowers, but told him not to take anything away with him.

All day he remained on the island, listening to the most ravishing music, and feasting and dancing with the Fairies.

When it came time for him to leave, he hid a flower in his bosom, for he wished to show it to his friends at home. He then said farewell to the Fairies, and returned through the dark passage to the margin of the lake. But when he put his hand in his bosom to pull out the flower, he found to his amazement that it had vanished. At the same moment he fell insensible to the ground.

When he came to himself, the door in the rock had disappeared. And though he searched day after day, he never again found the passage to the Fairy Island.

THE FOUR-LEAVED CLOVER

From Cornwall

Some years ago, in Cornwall, there was a farmer who owned a fine red cow, named Rosy. She gave twice as much milk as any ordinary cow. Even in Winter, when other cows were reduced to skin and bone, Rosy kept in good condition, and yielded richer milk than ever.

One Spring, Rosy continued to give plenty of milk every morning, but at night, when Molly the maid tried to milk her, she kicked the bucket over and galloped away across the field. This happened night after night, and such behaviour was so strange, that Dame Pendar, the farmer's wife, decided to see what she could do. But no sooner did she try to milk Rosy than the cow put up her foot, kicked the bucket to bits, and raced away, bellowing, tail-on-end.

During this Spring the farmer's cattle and fields thrived wonderfully. And so things continued until May Day. Now, on May Day night, when Molly attempted, as usual, to milk Rosy, she was surprised to see the cow stand quietly and to hear her begin to moo gently; and, more wonderful still, the pail was soon full of foaming new milk. Molly rose from her stool, and, pulling a handful of grass, rolled it into a pad, and tucked it in her hat, so that she might the more easily carry the bucket on her head.

She put the hat on again, when what was her amazement to see whole swarms of little Fairies running around Rosy, while others were on her back, neck, and head, and still others were under her, holding up clover blossoms and buttercups in which to catch the streams of milk that flowed from her udder. The little Fairies moved around so swiftly that Molly's head grew dizzy as she watched them. Rosy seemed pleased. She tried to lick the Little People. They tickled her behind the horns, ran up and down her back, smoothing each hair or chasing away the flies. And after all the Fairies had drunk their fill, they brought armfuls of clover and grass to Rosy; and she ate it all, and lowed for more.

Molly stood with her bucket on her head, like one spell-bound, watching the Little People; and she would have continued to stand there, but Dame Pendar, the farmer's wife, called her loudly to know why she had not brought the milk, if there was any.

At the first sound of Dame Pendar's voice, all the Fairies pointed their fingers at Molly, and made such wry faces that she was frightened almost to death. Then—*whisk!* and they were gone!

Molly hurried to the house, and told her mistress, and her master, too, all that she had seen.

"Surely," said Dame Pendar, "you must have a Four-leaved Clover somewhere about you. Give me the wad of grass in your hat."

Molly took it out, and gave it to her; and sure enough there was the Four-leaved Clover which had opened Molly's eyes on that May Day.

As for Rosy, she kicked up her heels, and, bellowing like mad, galloped away. Over meadows and moors she went racing and roaring, and was never seen again.

THE GILLIE DHU

From Scotland

Once upon a time a little girl, named Jessie, was wandering in the wood, and lost her way. It was Summer time, and the air was warm. She wandered on and on, trying to find her way home, but she could not find the path out of the wood. Twilight came, and weary and footsore she sat down under a fir tree, and began to cry.

"Why are you crying, little girl?" said a voice behind her.

Jessie looked around, and saw a pretty little man dressed in moss and green leaves. His eyes were dark as dark, and his hair was black as black, and his mouth was large and showed a hundred white teeth as small as seed pearls. He was smiling merrily, and his cream-yellow cheeks were dimpled, and his eyes soft and kindly. Indeed, he seemed so friendly that Jessie quite forgot to be afraid.

"Why are you crying, little girl?" he asked again. "Your teardrops are falling like dew on the blue flowers at your feet!"

"I've lost my way," sobbed Jessie, "and the night is coming on."

"Do not cry, little girl," said he gently. "I will lead you through the wood. I know every path—the rabbit's path, the hare's path, the fox's path, the goat's path, the path of the deer, and the path of men."

"Oh, thank you! Thank you!" exclaimed Jessie, as she looked the tiny man up and down, and wondered to see his strange clothes.

"Where do you dwell, little girl?" asked he.

So Jessie told him, and he said: "You have been walking every way but the right way. Follow me, and you'll reach home before the stars come out to peep at us through the trees."

Then he turned around, and began to trip lightly in front of her, and she followed on. He went so fast that she feared she might lose sight of him, but he turned around again and again and smiled and beckoned. And when he saw that she was still far behind, he danced and twirled about until she came up. Then he scampered on as before.

At length Jessie reached the edge of the wood, and, oh, joy! there was her father's house beside the blue lake. Then the little man, smiling, bade her good-bye.

"Have I not led you well?" said he. "Do not forget me. I am the Gillie Dhu from Fairyland. I love little girls and boys. If you are ever lost in the wood again, I will come and help you! Good-bye, little girl! Good-bye!"

And laughing merrily, he trotted away, and was soon lost to sight among the trees.

HOW KAHUKURA LEARNED
TO MAKE NETS

From New Zealand

Once upon a time there lived a man named Kahukura. One evening, when he was on his way to a distant village, he came to a lonely spot on the seashore. As he was walking slowly along, he saw a large pile of the heads and tails of fishes lying the on beach. Now, in those days men had no nets and were obliged to catch fish with spears and hooks; and when Kahukura saw the pile he was very much astonished.

"Who has had such luck!" he exclaimed. "It is hard to catch one fish! Here must be the heads and tails of a thousand!"

Then he looked closely at the footprints in the sand. "No mortals have been fishing here!" he cried. "Fairies must have done this! I will watch to-night and see what they do."

So when darkness came, he returned to the spot, and hid behind a rock. He waited a long time, and at last he saw a fleet of tiny canoes come spinning over the waves. They ranged themselves in a line at a distance from the shore, and Kahukura could see many little figures in them bending and pulling. He could even hear small voices shouting: "The net here! The net there!" Then the little figures dropped something overboard, and began to haul it toward the shore, singing very sweetly the while.

When the canoes drew near land, Kahukura saw that each was crowded with Fairies. They all sprang out upon the beach, and began to drag ashore a great net filled with fishes.

While the Fairies were struggling with the net Kahukura joined them, and hauled away at a rope. He was a very fair man, so that his skin seemed almost as white as the Fairies', and they did not notice him. So he pulled away, and pulled away, and soon the net was landed.

The Fairies ran forward to divide the catch. It was just at the peep of dawn, and they hurried to take all the fish they could carry, each Fairy stringing his share by running a twig through the gills. And as they strung the fish they kept calling out to one another:—

"Hurry! hurry! We must finish before the sun rises."

Kahukura had a short string with a knot in the end, and he strung his share on it, until it was filled. But when he lifted the string the knot gave way, and all the fish slid to the ground. Then some of the Fairies ran forward to help him, and tied the knot. Again he filled the string and all the fish slid off, and again the Fairies tied the knot.

Meanwhile day began to break over the sea, and the sun to rise. Then the Fairies saw Kahukura's face, and knew that he was a man. They gave little cries of terror. They ran this way and that in confusion. They left their fish and canoes, they abandoned their net. And shrieking they all vanished over the sea.

Kahukura, seeing that he was alone, made haste to examine the canoes. They were only the stems of flax! He lifted the net. It was woven of rushes curiously tied. He carried it home, and made some like it for his neighbours. After that he taught his children how to weave nets. And so, say the Maori folk, they all learned to make nets. And from that day to this they have caught many fish.

ECHO, THE CAVE FAIRY

From the Island of Mangaia

In the very long ago, Rangi the Brave came from the Land-of-the-Bright-Parrot-Feathers to the Island of Mangaia. Swiftly over the blue waves sped his canoe. He stepped out upon the land, and lay down to rest in the shade of a broad-leaved tree covered with gorgeous blooms. And after he had slept and was refreshed, he arose and wandered about the island.

Beautiful was the place with cocoa palms waving their tall fronds in the air, and with banana trees heavy with golden fruit. But though Rangi walked all that day and the next, he saw no human being. He heard no sounds except the beat of the sea against the shore, and the whirring of hundreds of bright-winged birds that passed like flashes of blue, green, and crimson, from tree to tree, and from grove to grove. Softly the perfumed breezes fanned his cheek, and played in his hair.

"Like a lovely dream is this island!" thought he, "but as lonely as the sea on a moonlit night!"

Then to comfort himself he threw back his head and called: "Halloo! Halloo!"

And from a pile of rocks overhanging a deep gorge, a voice answered: "Halloo!"

"Who art thou?" cried Rangi in wonder. "What is thy name?"

And the voice answered more softly: "What is thy name?"

"Where art thou? Where art thou hidden?" he shouted.

And the voice answered mockingly: "Where art thou hidden?"

Then Rangi in anger shouted fiercely: "Accursed be thou, hide-and-seek spirit!"

And the voice screamed back as in derision: "Accursed be thou!"

Thereupon Rangi grasped his spear tighter, and strode toward the rocks, determined to punish the insolent one. Leaping from boulder to boulder, he entered the gorge. And ever as he proceeded, he shouted threats; and ever the mocking voice answered from some distant spot.

The gorge grew darker and narrower, until Rangi suddenly found himself in a wide-mouthed cavern. Its walls and roof glittered with pendant crystals from which fell, drop by drop, clear water like dew. A white mist rose from the rocky floor, and through it Rangi saw dimly a lovely Fairy face gazing roguishly at him. It was wreathed in rippling hair, and crowned with flowers. Archly it smiled, then melted away in the mist.

"Who art thou?" whispered Rangi in awe. "Art thou Echo indeed?"

And from the glittering walls and roof came a thousand sweet answers:—

"Echo indeed!"

VIII. *Away! Away! To Fairyland!*

THE MAGIC FERNS

From Cornwall

Not many years since there lived in Cornwall a pretty young girl named Cherry. As she and her mother were poor, Cherry determined to go out to service. So one morning early, she took her little bundle of clothes, and started out to find a place with some respectable family. She walked until she came to four cross-roads, and, not knowing which to follow, she sat down on a boulder to think.

The spot where she sat was covered with beautiful ferns that curled their delicate fronds over the boulder. And while she was lost in thought, she unconsciously picked a few fronds and crushed them in her hand.

Immediately she heard a strange voice at her elbow say:—

"My pretty young woman, what are you looking for?"

She glanced up, and saw standing near her a handsome young man, who was holding a bunch of the ferns.

"I am looking for a place, sir," said she.

"And what kind of a place do you wish?" asked he, with a sweet and winning smile.

"I am not particular," answered she. "I can make myself generally useful."

"Indeed!" said the stranger. "And do you think you could look after one little boy?"

"That I'd love to do!" said she, smiling.

"Then," replied he, "I wish to hire you for a year and a day. My home is not far from here. Will you go with me, Cherry, and see it?"

Cherry stared in astonishment to hear him speak her name; and he added:—

"Oh! I see you thought that I did not know you! I watched you

100

one day while you were dressing your hair beside one of my ponds; and I saw you pluck some of my sweetest-scented violets to put in those lovely tresses! but will you go with me, Cherry?"

"For a year and a day?" asked she.

"You need not be alarmed," said he very kindly. "Just kiss the fern leaf that is in your hand, and say:—

'For a year and a day
I promise to stay!'"

"Is that all!" said Cherry. So she kissed the fern leaf, and said the words as he told her to.

Instantly the young man passed the bunch of ferns that he held over both her eyes. The ground in front of her seemed to open; and, though she did not feel herself move from the boulder where she sat, yet she knew that she was going down rapidly into the earth.

"Here we are, Cherry," said the young man. "Is there a tear of sorrow under your eyelid? If so, let me wipe it away, for no human tear can enter our dwelling."

And as he spoke he brushed Cherry's eyes with the fern leaves. And, lo! before her was such a country as she had never dreamed of!

Hills and valleys were covered with flowers strangely brilliant, so that the whole country appeared to be sown with gems that glittered in a light as clear as that of the Summer sun, yet as mild as moonshine. There were glimmering rivers, and singing waterfalls, and sparkling fountains; while everywhere beautiful little ladies and gentlemen, dressed in green and gold, were walking, or sitting on banks of flowers. Oh! it was a wonderful world!

"Here we are at home!" said the young man—and strangely enough he was changed! He had become the handsomest little man Cherry had ever seen, and he wore a green silk coat covered with spangles of gold.

He led her into a noble mansion, the furniture of which was of ivory and pearl, inlaid with gold and silver and studded with emeralds. After passing through many rooms they came to one whose walls were hung with lace as fine as the finest cobwebs, and most beautifully twined with flowers. In the middle of the room was a cradle of wrought sea-shell, reflecting so many colours that Cherry could scarcely bear to look at it. The little man led her to this, and in it was lying asleep a little boy so beautiful that he ravished the sight.

"This is your charge," said the little man. "I am King of this country, and I wish my son to know something of human nature. You have nothing to do but to wash and dress the boy when he wakes, to take him walking in the garden, to tell him stories, and to put him to sleep when he is weary."

Cherry was delighted beyond words, for at first sight she loved the darling little boy. And when he woke, he seemed to love her just as dearly. She was very happy, and cared tenderly for him; and the time passed away with astonishing rapidity. In fact it seemed scarcely a week later, when she opened her eyes and found everything about her changed. Indeed, there she was lying in her own bed in her mother's cottage!

She heard her mother calling her name with joy; and the neighbours came crowding around her bed. It was just one year and a day from the time when she had sat on the boulder, and had met the fine young man. She told her adventures to all, but they would not believe her. They shook their heads and went away, saying: "Poor Cherry is certainly mad!"

From that day on, she was never happy, but sat pining, and dreaming of the hour when she had picked the magic ferns. And though she often went back to the boulder, she never again saw the young man, nor found the way to Fairyland.

THE SMITH AND THE FAIRIES

From Scotland

Years ago there lived in Scotland an honest, hard-working smith. He had only one child, a boy, fourteen years of age, cheerful, strong, and healthy.

Suddenly the boy fell ill. He took to his bed, and moped away whole days. No one could tell what was the matter with him. Although he had a tremendous appetite, he wasted away, getting thin, yellow, and old.

At last one morning, while the smith was standing idly at his forge, with no heart for work, he was surprised to see a Wise-man, who lived at some distance, enter his shop. The smith hastened to tell him about his son, and to ask his advice.

The Wise-man listened gravely, then said: "The boy has been carried away by the Little People, and they have left a Changeling in his place."

"Alas! And what am I to do?" asked the smith. "How am I ever to see my own son again?"

"I will tell you how," answered the Wise-man. "But first, to make sure that it is not your own son you have, gather together all the egg-shells you can get. Go into the room where the boy is, and spread them out carefully before him. Then pour water in them, and carry them carefully in your hands, two by two. Carry them as though they were very heavy, and arrange them around the fireplace."

The smith, accordingly, collected as many egg-shells as he could find. He went into the room, and did as the Wise-man had said.

He had not been long at work, before there came from the bed where the boy lay, a great shout of laughter, and the boy cried out:—

"I am now eight hundred years old, and I have never seen the like of that before!"

103

The smith hurried back, and told this to the Wise-man.

"Did I not assure you," said the Wise-man, "that it is not your son whom you have? Your son is in a Fairy Mound not far from here. Get rid as soon as possible of this Changeling, and I think I may promise you your son again.

"You might light a very great and bright fire before the bed on which this stranger is lying. He will ask you why you are doing so. Answer him at once: 'You shall see presently when I lay you upon it.' If you do this, the Changeling will become frightened and fly through the roof."

The smith again followed the Wise-man's advice; kindled a blazing fire, and answered as he had been told to do. And, just as he was going to seize the Changeling and fling him on the fire, the thing gave an awful yell, and sprang through the roof.

The smith, overjoyed, returned to the Wise-man, and told this to him.

"On Midsummer Night," said the Wise-man, "the Fairy Mound, where your boy is kept, will open. You must provide yourself with a dirk and a crowing cock. Go to the Mound. You will hear singing and dancing and much merriment going on. At twelve o'clock a door in the Mound will open. Advance boldly. Enter this door, but first stick the dirk in the ground before it, to prevent the Mound from closing. You will find yourself in a spacious apartment, beautifully clean; and there working at a forge, you will see your son. The Fairies will then question you, and you must answer that you have come for your son, and will not go without him. Do this, and see what happens!"

Midsummer Night came, and the smith provided himself with a dirk and a crowing cock. He went to the Fairy Mound, and all happened as the Wise-man had said.

The Fairies came crowding around him, buzzing and pinching his legs; and when he said that he had come for his son, and would not go away without him, they all gave a loud laugh. At the same minute the cock, that was dozing in the smith's arms, woke up. It leaped to his shoulder, and, clapping its wings, crowed loud and long.

At that the Fairies were furious. They seized the smith and

his son and threw them out of the Mound, and pulled up the dirk and flung it after them. And in that instant all was dark.

For a year and a day the boy never spoke, nor would he do a turn of work. At last one morning as he was watching his father finish a sword, he exclaimed:—

"That's not the way to do it!"

And taking the tools from his father's hands, he set to work, and soon fashioned a glittering sharp sword, the like of which had never been seen before.

From that day on, the boy helped his father, and showed him how to make Fairy swords, and in a few years they both became rich and famous. And they always lived together contentedly and happily.

THE GIRL WHO WAS STOLEN
BY THE FAIRIES

From Ireland

Never go near an Elfin Mound on May Day. For in the month of May the Fairies are very powerful, and they wander about the meadows looking for pretty maidens to carry off to Fairyland.

One beautiful May Day in old Ireland, a young girl fell asleep at noonday on an Elfin Mound. The Fairies saw how pretty she was, so they carried her off to Fairyland, and left in her stead an image that looked exactly like her.

Evening fell, and as the girl did not return home, her mother sent the neighbours to look for her in all directions. They found the image, and, thinking that it was the girl herself, they carried it home, and laid it in her bed. But the image neither moved nor spoke, and lay there silently for two days.

On the morning of the third day an old Witch-woman entered the house, and looking at the image, said:—

"Your daughter is Fairy-struck. Rub this ointment on her forehead, and see what you shall see!"

Then the old woman placed a vial of green ointment in the mother's hand, and disappeared.

The mother immediately rubbed the forehead of the image, and the girl herself sat up in bed, weeping and wringing her hands.

"Oh, mother!" she cried. "Oh, why did you bring me back! I was so happy! I was in a beautiful palace where handsome Princesses and Princes were dancing to the sweetest music. They made me dance with them, and threw a mantle of rich gold over my shoulders. Now it is all gone, and I shall never see the beautiful palace any more!"

Then the mother wept, and said: "Oh, my child, stay with me!

I have no other daughter but you! And if the Fairies take you, I shall die!"

The girl wept loudly at this, and throwing her arms around her mother's neck, kissed her, and promised that she would not go near the Elfin Mound. And she kept her word, so she never saw the Fairies again.

THE GIRL WHO DANCED
WITH THE FAIRIES

From Ireland

One must never wander about alone on Hallowe'en, for then the Fairies are abroad looking for mortals to trick and lead astray.

Now, there was once a girl, the prettiest girl in all Ireland, who late one Hallowe'en was going to a spring to fetch some water. Her foot slipped, and she fell. When she got up, she looked about her, and saw that she was in a very strange place. A great fire was burning near, around which a number of people, beautifully dressed, were dancing.

A handsome young man, like a Prince, with a red sash, and a golden band in his hair, left the fire, and came toward her. He greeted her kindly, and asked her to dance.

"It is a foolish thing, sir, to ask me to dance," replied she, "since there is no music."

At that the young man lifted his hand, and instantly the most delicious music sounded. Then he took her by the fingers and drew her into the dance. Around and around they whirled, and they danced and danced until the moon and stars went down. And all the time, the girl seemed to float in the air and she forgot everything except the sweet music and the young man.

At last the dancing ceased, and a door opened in the earth. The young man, who seemed to be the King of all, led the girl down a pair of stairs, followed by all the gay company. At the end of a long passage they came to a hall bright and beautiful with gold and silver and lights. A table was covered with every good thing to eat, and wine was poured out in golden cups.

The young man lifted a cup, and offered it to the girl; at the same moment some one whispered in her ear:—

"Do not drink! Do not eat! If you do either, you will never see your home again!"

Well, the girl, when she heard that, set the cup down and refused to drink. Immediately all the company grew angry. A great buzzing arose. The lights went out. And the girl felt something grasp her, and rush her forth from the hall and up the stairs; and in a minute she found herself beside the spring holding her pitcher in her hand.

She did not wait for anything, but ran home as fast as she could, and locked herself in tight, and crept into bed. Then she heard a great clamour of little voices outside her door, and she could hear them cry:—

"The power we had over you to-night is gone, because you refused to drink! But wait until next Hallowe'en Night, when you dance with us on the hill! Then we shall keep you forever!—forever!"

ELIDORE AND THE GOLDEN BALL

From Wales

Once upon a time, in the land of Wales, near the fall of the Tawe into the sea, there lived a boy called Elidore. He was a bright lad, but so fond of play that he would not study at all. His teacher flogged him so often and so hard that one morning Elidore ran away from home, and hid under a hollow bank by the side of the river.

There he stayed two nights and two days, getting hungrier and thirstier every moment. At last, when it seemed as if he could stand his sufferings no longer, he saw a little door open in the side of the bank and two Elfin Men step out. They stood before him, and, bowing low, said:—

"Come with us, dear boy, and we will lead you to a land full of delights and sports, where you may play all the time."

Elidore was overjoyed. He rose and followed the Elfin Men through the door. They conducted him down a long, dark passage through the hill. At length they came out into a beautiful country adorned with singing crystal streams and flowery meadows. But it was always twilight there, for the light of the sun, moon, and stars could not reach that land.

The Elfin Men led Elidore to a golden palace, and presented him to the King of the Elves, who was seated upon his throne and was surrounded by a train of little people richly clad. The King questioned Elidore kindly, then, calling his eldest son, the Elfin Prince, bade him take the earth-boy and make him happy.

So Elidore dwelt in Elfinland, and day after day was fed with milk and saffron; and he played with the Elfin Prince, tossing gold and silver balls. When he walked in the meadows to pick flowers, he saw everywhere about him the Elfin people, with long, flowing yellow hair, riding on little horses and chasing tiny deer with Fairy hounds. For all the people in Elfinland played and rode about night and day, and they never worked. Sometimes on moonlit nights they rode through the dark passage to the upper world, and danced in Fairy Rings on the grass. And when they went to their dances, they took Elidore with them.

After Elidore had lived in Elfinland for some time, the King permitted him one moonlit night to go alone through the dark passage to visit his mother. He did so, and she was delighted to see him, for she had thought him dead. He told her about the wonders of Elfinland, and how he was fed on milk and saffron, and played with gold and silver toys. She begged him, the next time he came, to bring her a bit of Fairy Gold. He promised to do so, and returned to Elfinland.

It so happened, one day soon after this, that Elidore was playing with the Elfin Prince. He snatched a beautiful golden ball from the Prince's hands, and hastened with it through the dark passage. As he ran he heard behind him the shouts of many angry Elves and the sound of their horses' hoofs, and the barking of the Fairy dogs; and knew that he was being pursued.

Faster he ran in terror, but nearer came the patter of a thousand little feet, and the Elfin shouts. Still more terrified, he rushed through the door in the hill and sped homeward. As he sprang into his mother's house his foot caught, and he fell over the threshold. At the same moment two Elves, who had outrun the others, leaped over him and snatched the golden ball from his hands.

"Thief!" "Robber!" "Thief!" they screamed, and vanished.

As for Elidore, he rose up too ashamed to eat or sleep that night. The next day he went to the river bank and searched for the door, but could find no trace of it. And though he searched every day for a year, he never again found the entrance to Elfinland.

But from that time he was a changed boy. He studied hard, loved truth, and hated lying and stealing. And, when he grew up, he became a great man in Wales.

IX. *Fairy Godmothers and Wonderful Gifts*

PRINCE CHÉRI

Madame Le Prince de Beaumont
(After Miss Mulock)

Long ago there lived a monarch, who was such a very honest man that his subjects entitled him "the Good King." One day when he was out hunting, a little white rabbit, which had been half killed by his hounds, leaped right into His Majesty's arms. Said he, caressing it, "This poor creature has put itself under my protection, and I will allow no one to injure it." So he carried it to his palace, had prepared for it a neat little rabbit-hutch, with abundance of the daintiest food, such as rabbits love, and there he left it.

The same night, when he was alone in his chamber, there appeared to him a beautiful lady. She was dressed neither in gold nor silver nor brocade; but her flowing robes were white as snow, and she wore a garland of white roses on her head. The Good King was greatly astonished at the sight, for his door was locked, and he wondered how so dazzling a lady could possibly enter; but she soon removed his doubts.

"I am the Fairy Candide," said she, with a smiling and gracious air. "Passing through the wood, where you were hunting, I took a desire to know if you were as good as men say you are. I therefore changed myself into a white rabbit, and sought refuge in your arms. You saved me; and now I know that those who are merciful to dumb beasts will be ten times more so to human beings. You merit the name your subjects give you: you are the Good King. I thank you for your protection, and shall be always one of your best friends. You have but to say what you most desire, and I promise you your wish shall be granted."

"Madam," replied the King, "if you are a Fairy, you must

know, without my telling you, the wish of my heart. I have one well-beloved son, Prince Chéri: whatever kindly feeling you have toward me, extend it to him."

"Willingly," said Candide. "I will make him the handsomest, richest, or most powerful Prince in the world. Choose whichever you desire for him."

"None of the three," returned the father. "I only wish him to be good—the best Prince in the world. Of what use would riches, power, or beauty be to him if he were a bad man?"

"You are right," said the Fairy; "but I cannot make him good: he must do that himself. I can only change his external fortunes. For his personal character, the utmost I can promise is to give good counsel, reprove him for his faults, and even punish him, if he will not punish himself. You mortals can do the same with your children."

"Ah, yes!" said the King, sighing.

Still, he felt that the kindness of a Fairy was something gained for his son, and died not long after, content and at peace.

Prince Chéri mourned deeply, for he dearly loved his father, and would have gladly given all his kingdoms and treasures to keep him in life a little longer.

Two days after the Good King was no more, Prince Chéri was sleeping in his chamber, when he saw the same dazzling vision of the Fairy Candide.

"I promised your father," said she, "to be your best friend, and in pledge of this take what I now give you." And she placed a small gold ring upon his finger. "Poor as it looks, it is more precious than diamonds; for whenever you do ill it will prick your finger. If after that warning you still continue in evil, you will lose my friendship, and I shall become your direst enemy."

So saying she disappeared, leaving Chéri in such amazement that he would have believed it all a dream, save for the ring on his finger.

He was for a long time so good that the ring never pricked him at all; and this made him so cheerful and pleasant in his humour that everybody called him "Happy Prince Chéri." But one unlucky day he was out hunting and found no sport, which vexed him so much that he showed his ill-temper by his looks and ways. He fancied his ring felt very tight and uncomfortable, but as it did not prick him, he took no heed of this; until, reën-tering his palace, his little pet dog, Bibi, jumped up upon him, and was sharply told to get away. The creature, accustomed to nothing but caresses, tried to attract his attention by pulling at his garments, when Prince Chéri turned and gave it a severe kick. At this moment he felt in his finger a prick like a pin.

"What nonsense!" said he to himself. "The Fairy must be making game of me. Why, what great evil have I done? I, the master of a great empire, cannot I kick my own dog?"

A voice replied, or else Prince Chéri imagined it: "No, sire; the master of a great empire has a right to do good, but not evil. I—a Fairy—am as much above you as you are above your dog. I might punish you, kill you, if I chose; but I prefer leaving you to amend your ways. You have been guilty of three faults to-day—bad temper, passion, cruelty. Do better to-morrow."

The Prince promised, and kept his word awhile; but he had been brought up by a foolish nurse, who indulged him in every way, and was always telling him that he would be a King one day, when he might do as he liked in all things. He found out now that even a King cannot always do that; it vexed him, and made him angry. His ring began to prick him so often that his little finger was continually bleeding. He disliked this, as was natural, and soon began to consider whether it would not be easier to throw the ring away altogether than to be constantly annoyed by it. It was such a queer thing for a King to have always a spot of blood on his finger!

At last, unable to put up with it any more, he took his ring off, and hid it where he would never see it; and believed himself the happiest of men, for he could now do exactly what he liked. He did it, and became every day more and more miserable.

One day he saw a young girl, so beautiful that, being always accustomed to have his own way, he immediately determined to marry her. He never doubted that she would be only too glad to be made a Queen, for she was very poor. But Zelia—that was her name—answered, to his great astonishment, that she would rather not marry him.

"Do I displease you?" asked the Prince, into whose mind it had never entered that he could displease anybody.

"Not at all, my Prince," said the honest peasant-maiden. "You are very handsome, very charming; but you are not like your father the Good King. I will not be your Queen, for you would make me miserable."

At these words the Prince's love seemed all to turn to hatred. He gave orders to his guards to convey Zelia to a prison near the palace, and then took counsel with his foster-brother, the one of all his ill companions who most incited him to do wrong.

"Sir," said this man, "if I were in Your Majesty's place, I would never vex myself about a poor silly girl. Feed her on bread and water till she comes to her senses; and if she still refuses you, let her die in torment, as a warning to your other subjects should they venture to dispute your will. You will be disgraced should you suffer yourself to be conquered by a simple girl."

"But," said Prince Chéri, "shall I not be disgraced if I harm a creature so perfectly innocent?"

"No one is innocent who disputes Your Majesty's authority," said the courtier, bowing; "and it is better to commit an injustice than allow it to be supposed you can ever be contradicted with impunity."

This touched Chéri on his weak point—his good impulses faded. He resolved once more to ask Zelia if she would marry him, and, if she again refused, to sell her as a slave. Arrived at the cell in which she was confined, what was his astonishment to find her gone! He knew not whom to accuse, for he had kept the key in his pocket the whole time. At last, the foster-brother suggested that the escape of Zelia might have been contrived by an old man, Suliman by name, the Prince's former tutor, who was the only one who now ventured to blame him for anything that he did. Chéri sent immediately, and ordered his old friend to be brought to him, loaded heavily with irons.

Then, full of fury, he went and shut himself up in his own chamber, where he went raging to and fro, till startled by a noise like a clap of thunder. The Fairy Candide stood before him.

"Prince," said she, in a severe voice, "I promised your father to give you good counsels, and to punish you if you refused to follow them. My counsels were forgotten, my punishments despised. Under the figure of a man, you have been no better than the beasts you chase: like a lion in fury, a wolf in gluttony, a serpent in revenge, and a bull in brutality. Take, therefore, in your new form the likeness of all these animals."

Scarcely had Prince Chéri heard these words, than to his horror he found himself transformed into what the Fairy had named. He was a creature with the head of a lion, the horns of a bull, the feet of a wolf, and the tail of a serpent. At the same time he felt himself transported to a distant forest, where, standing on the bank of a stream, he saw reflected in the water his own frightful shape, and heard a voice saying:—

"Look at thyself, and know thy soul has become a thousand times uglier even than thy body."

Chéri recognized the voice of Candide, and in his rage would have sprung upon her and devoured her; but he saw nothing, and the same voice said behind him:—

"Cease thy feeble fury, and learn to conquer thy pride by being in submission to thine own subjects."

Hearing no more, he soon quitted the stream, hoping at least to get rid of the sight of himself; but he had scarcely gone twenty paces when he tumbled into a pitfall that was laid to catch bears. The bear-hunters, descending from some trees hard by, caught him, chained him, and only too delighted to get hold of such a curious-looking animal, led him along with them to the capital of his own Kingdom.

There great rejoicings were taking place, and the bear-hunters, asking what it was all about, were told that it was because Prince Chéri, the torment of his subjects, had been struck dead by a thunderbolt—just punishment of all his crimes. Four courtiers, his wicked companions, had wished to divide his throne among them; but the people had risen up against them, and offered the crown to Suliman, the old tutor whom Chéri had ordered to be arrested.

All this the poor monster heard. He even saw Suliman sitting upon his own throne, and trying to calm the populace by representing to them that it was not certain Prince Chéri was dead; that he might return one day to reassume with honour the crown which Suliman only consented to wear as a sort of viceroy.

"I know his heart," said the honest and faithful old man; "it is tainted, but not corrupt. If alive, he may reform yet, and be all his father over again to you, his people, whom he has caused to suffer so much."

These words touched the poor beast so deeply that he ceased to beat himself against the iron bars of the cage in which the hunters carried him about, became gentle as a lamb, and suffered himself to be taken quietly to a menagerie, where were kept all sorts of strange and ferocious animals—a place which he had himself often visited as a boy, but never thought he should be shut up there himself.

However, he owned he had deserved it all, and began to make amends by showing himself very obedient to his keeper. This man was almost as great a brute as the animals he had charge of, and when he was in ill-humour he used to beat them without rhyme or reason. One day, while he was sleeping, a tiger broke loose and leaped upon him, eager to devour him. Chéri at first felt a thrill of pleasure at the thought of being revenged; then, seeing how helpless the man was, he wished himself free, that he might defend him. Immediately the doors of his cage opened.

The keeper, waking up, saw the strange beast leap out, and imagined, of course, that he was going to be slain at once. Instead, he saw the tiger lying dead, and the strange beast creeping up and laying itself at his feet to be caressed. But as he lifted up his hand to stroke it, a voice was heard saying, "Good actions never go unrewarded." And, instead of the frightful monster, there crouched on the ground nothing but a pretty little dog.

Chéri, delighted to find himself thus transformed, caressed the keeper in every possible way, till at last the man took him up into his arms and carried him to the King, to whom he related this wonderful story from beginning to end. The Queen wished to have the charming little dog; and Chéri would have been exceedingly happy, could he have forgotten that he was originally a man and a King. He was lodged most elegantly, had the richest of collars to adorn his neck, and heard himself praised continually. But his beauty rather brought him into trouble, for the Queen, afraid lest he might grow too large for a pet, took advice of dog-doctors, who ordered that he should be fed entirely upon bread, and that very sparingly; so poor Chéri was sometimes nearly starved.

One day, when they gave him his crust for breakfast, a fancy seized him to go and eat it in the palace-garden; so he took the bread in his mouth, and trotted away toward a stream which he knew, and where he sometimes stopped to drink. But instead of the stream he saw a splendid palace, glittering with gold and precious stones. Entering the doors was a crowd of men and women, magnificently dressed; and within there was singing and dancing, and good cheer of all sorts. Yet, however grandly and gaily the people went in, Chéri noticed that those who came out were pale, thin, ragged, half-naked, covered with wounds and sores. Some of them dropped dead at once; others dragged themselves on a little way and then lay down, dying of hunger, and vainly begged a morsel of bread from others who were entering in—who never took the least notice of them.

Chéri perceived one woman, who was trying feebly to gather and eat some green herbs. "Poor thing!" said he to himself; "I know what it is to be hungry, and I want my breakfast badly enough; but still it will not kill me to wait till dinner-time, and my crust may save the life of this poor woman."

So the little dog ran up to her, and dropped his bread at her feet; she picked it up, and ate it with avidity. Soon she looked quite recovered, and Chéri, delighted, was trotting back again to his kennel, when he heard loud cries, and saw a young girl dragged by four men to the door of the palace, which they were trying to compel her to enter. Oh, how he wished himself a monster again, as when he slew the tiger! For the young girl was no other than his beloved Zelia. Alas! what could a poor little dog do to defend her? But he ran forward and barked at the men and bit their heels, until at last they chased him away with heavy blows. And then he lay down outside the palace-door, determined to watch and see what had become of Zelia.

Conscience pricked him now. "What!" he thought, "I am furious against these wicked men, who are carrying her away; and did I not do the same myself? Did I not cast her into prison, and intend to sell her as a slave? Who knows how much more wickedness I might not have done to her and others, if Heaven's justice had not stopped me in time?"

While he lay thinking and repenting, he heard a window open, and saw Zelia throw out of it a bit of dainty meat. Chéri, who felt hungry enough by this time, was just about to eat it, when the woman to whom he had given his crust snatched him up in her arms.

"Poor little beast!" cried she, patting him, "every bit of food in that palace is poisoned; you shall not touch a morsel."

And at the same time the voice in the air repeated again, "Good actions never go unrewarded." And Chéri found himself changed into a beautiful little white pigeon. He remembered with joy that white was the colour of the Fairy Candide, and began to hope that she was taking him into favour again.

So he stretched his wings, delighted that he might now have a chance of approaching his fair Zelia. He flew up to the palace windows, and, finding one of them open, entered and sought everywhere, but he could not find Zelia. Then, in despair, he flew out again, resolved to go over the world until he beheld her once more.

He took flight at once, and traversed many countries, swiftly as a bird can, but found no trace of his beloved. At length in a desert, sitting beside an old hermit in his cave and partaking with him of his frugal repast, Chéri saw a poor peasant girl and recognized Zelia. Transported with joy, he flew in, perched on her shoulder, and expressed his delight and affection by a thousand caresses.

She, charmed with the pretty little pigeon, caressed it in her turn, and promised it that, if it would stay with her, she would love it always.

"What have you done, Zelia?" said the hermit, smiling. And while he spoke the white pigeon vanished, and there stood Prince Chéri in his own natural form. "Your enchantment ended, Prince, when Zelia promised to love you. Indeed, she has loved you always, but your many faults constrained her to hide her love. These are now amended, and you may both live happy if you will, because your union is founded upon mutual esteem."

Chéri and Zelia threw themselves at the feet of the hermit, whose form also began to change. His soiled garments became of dazzling whiteness, and his long beard and withered face grew into the flowing hair and lovely countenance of Fairy Candide.

"Rise up, my children," said she; "I must now transport you to your palace, and restore to Prince Chéri his father's crown, of which he is now worthy."

She had scarcely ceased speaking when they found themselves in the chamber of Suliman, who, delighted to find again his beloved pupil and master, willingly resigned the throne, and became the most faithful of his subjects.

King Chéri and Queen Zelia reigned together for many years, and it is said that the former was so blameless and strict in all his duties that, though he constantly wore the ring which Candide had restored to him, it never once pricked his finger enough to make it bleed.

TOADS AND DIAMONDS

Charles Perrault

Once upon a time there was a widow who had two daughters. The elder was so exactly like her mother in disposition and in face that whoever saw one, saw the other. They were both so disagreeable and so proud that nobody could endure them.

The younger was the image of her dead father. She was sweet and kind-hearted, besides being very beautiful. While her mother loved the elder daughter to distraction, she hated the younger. The poor child had to eat in the kitchen, and work day and night. And twice every day she had to walk several miles to a distant fountain to fetch home a large pitcher of water.

One morning, while she was resting beside the fountain, a poor woman passing by, stopped and asked her for a drink.

"Yes, indeed!" said the obliging young girl. And immediately dipping her pitcher, she filled it where the water was coldest, and held it carefully up so that the woman might easily drink from it.

When the woman had finished drinking, she said: "You are so beautiful, so good, and so kind, that I must bestow a gift upon you. For every word that you speak, there shall fall from your lips either a flower or a jewel."

Now the woman was not really a poor peasant, but a Fairy who had taken that form in order to find how kind-hearted the young girl was. She then vanished.

As soon as the daughter arrived at home, her mother scolded her for being absent so long.

"I beg your pardon, my mother, for being gone such a long time," answered the girl. And as she spoke there fell from her lips three roses, three lilies, three pearls, and three large diamonds.

"What do I see!" exclaimed her mother in amazement. "Where did you get them, my child?" It was the first time in her life that she had ever called her "my child." "I do believe those jewels came from your mouth!"

The poor girl told her in a few words what had happened, and while she was talking a shower of blossoms and gems fell to the ground.

"Truly!" exclaimed the mother; "I must send my darling there! Look!" called she to the elder daughter; "see what comes out of your sister's mouth. Would you not be glad to have the same Fairy gifts? You have only to go and draw some water from the fountain, and when a poor woman asks for a drink to give it to her very politely."

"It would certainly look fine for me to carry a great pitcher to the fountain!" answered the elder daughter angrily.

"I wish you to go there at once," said her mother.

So the girl went, but grumbling. She took the prettiest silver pitcher that there was in the house; and she was no sooner arrived at the fountain than she saw, stepping out of the wood, a magnificent lady attired in rich robes. She approached the girl and asked her for a drink. It was the same Fairy who had appeared to her sister, but who had taken the form of a Princess in order to find how rude the girl would be.

"Oh, indeed!" answered the insolent girl; "do you think that I am come here on purpose to give you a drink? I suppose you think that I have brought a silver pitcher expressly to draw water for you! Draw the water yourself, my fine lady!"

"You are rude," replied the Fairy without becoming in the least angry. "Since you are so utterly disobliging, I bestow on you a gift. It is this, for every word that you speak, there shall fall from your mouth either a viper or a toad."

Then the Fairy vanished.

When her mother saw the girl returning, she cried out: "Well, my daughter!"

"Well, my mother!" snapped the hateful girl, and as she spoke there sprang from her mouth two snakes and one toad.

"What do I see!" shrieked her mother. "Your sister is the cause of this, and she shall pay for it!"

And she rushed to beat the poor child, who fled into the neighbouring wood. The son of the King was returning from the chase, and met her as she was running away. Seeing how beautiful she was, he asked her why she was there alone, and why she wept.

"Ah, sir," she said, "it is because my mother has driven me from home."

The King's son, seeing five or six pearls and as many diamonds fall from her lips, begged her to explain how such a marvel could be. When she told him about the Fairy's gift, he thought that such a wedding portion was more than he could expect with a Princess, so he led the girl to his palace, and married her.

As for the sister, she made herself so hated, and so many vipers and toads sprang from her mouth, that at last her mother drove her from home. And, after having been refused shelter by all the neighbours, she died in a dark corner of the wood.

BLANCHE AND ROSE

Madame Le Prince de Beaumont

Once upon a time there was a poor widow, who had two charming daughters. She named the elder Blanche, and the younger Rose, because they had the most beautiful complexions in the world.

One day, while the mother sat spinning at the door of her cottage, she saw a poor, bent, old woman hobbling by on a crutch. She pitied her, and said:—

"You are very tired. Sit down a minute and rest."

Then she called her daughters to fetch a chair. They both hastened, but Rose ran faster than her sister and brought it.

"Will you not have a drink?" asked the mother kindly.

"Indeed, I will," replied the old woman. "And it seems to me that I could eat a morsel, too, if you will give me something to strengthen me."

"I will gladly give you all that I have," said the mother, "but as I am poor, it will not be much."

Then she bade her daughters wait on the old woman, who had seated herself at the table. She told Blanche to go and pick some plums from the plum tree that Blanche herself had planted, and of which she was very proud. But instead of obeying her mother pleasantly, she went away grumbling, and thinking, "What a shame that I have taken such care of my tree just for this greedy old woman!" However, she did not dare refuse to fetch some plums, and she brought them with a very bad grace, and evidently much against her will.

"And you, Rose," said the mother, "you have no fruit to give this good lady, for your grapes are not yet ripe!"

"That is true," answered Rose, "but I hear my hen cackling. She has just laid an egg, and I will give that with all my heart!"

And without allowing the old woman time to speak, Rose ran out to seek the egg. But when she came back, the old woman had disappeared, and in her place stood the most beautiful lady—a Fairy.

"Good woman," said she to the mother, "I am about to reward your two daughters as they deserve. The elder shall become a great Queen, and the younger shall be a farmer's wife."

Then the lady waved a wand and in a twinkling the little cottage was changed into a pretty farmhouse surrounded by a flourishing farm.

"This is your wedding portion," said she to Rose. "I know I am giving to each of you what you like best."

So saying the Fairy disappeared, leaving the mother and daughters speechless with surprise and joy. They were delighted with the spotlessness of all the furniture. The chairs were of wood, but they were so well polished that they shone like mirrors. The beds were covered with linen as white as snow. In the stables there were twenty sheep, as many lambs, four oxen, four cows; and in the yard were chickens, ducks, and pigeons. There was also a pretty garden full of fruits and flowers.

Blanche saw without jealousy all that the Fairy had given her sister. She was taken up with the thought of the delightful times she should have when she became a Queen. Just then a party of royal hunters passed by. And while she stood in the door to look at them, she appeared so wonderfully beautiful in the eyes of the King that he determined to marry her.

After she became Queen, she said to Rose: "I do not wish you to be a farmer's wife. Come with me, sister, and I will wed you to a great lord."

"I am much obliged to you, my sister," answered Rose, "but I am used to the country, and wish always to remain here."

During the first months of her marriage Queen Blanche was so occupied with fine clothes, balls, and the theatre, that she thought of nothing else. But afterward she became accustomed to the gay doings of the Court, and nothing amused her. On the contrary, she had many troubles.

At first the courtiers paid her great deference, but she knew that when she was not present, they said to each other: "See how this little peasant puts on the airs of a fine lady! The King must have very low taste to choose such a wife!"

Talk like this came to the King, and he began to think that he had made a mistake in marrying Blanche, so he ceased to love her, and neglected her sadly. When the courtiers saw this, they no longer did her honour. She had not one true friend to whom she might confide her sorrows. She always had a doctor near her who examined her food and took away everything she liked. They put no salt in her soups. She was forbidden to walk when she wished to. In a word, she was interfered with from morning to night. The King took her children from her, and gave them in charge of governesses who brought them up badly. But the Queen dared not say a word.

Poor Blanche! She was dying of grief. She became so thin that everybody pitied her. She had not seen her sister for several years, because she thought that it would disgrace a Queen to visit a farmer's wife. But now feeling herself so unhappy, she asked the King's permission to pass a few days in the country. He gladly gave his consent, for he was delighted to be rid of her.

When she arrived in the evening at the home of Rose, a band of shepherds and shepherdesses were dancing gaily on the grass. "There was a time," sighed Blanche, "when I amused myself like these simple people! Then there was no one to prevent it!"

While she was thinking thus, her sister ran to embrace her, looking so happy and plump that Blanche could not help weeping as she gazed at her.

Rose had married a young farmer, who loved her dearly; and together they managed the farm that was the Fairy's marriage portion. Rose had not many servants, but those she had she treated so kindly that they were as devoted to her as if they were her children. Her neighbours, too, were so fond of her that they were always trying to show it. She had not much money, but she had no need of it, for her farm produced wheat, wine, and oil; her flocks furnished milk; and she made butter and cheese. She spun the wool of her sheep into clothing for her household, all of whom enjoyed the best of health. When the day's work was done, the whole family amused themselves with games, music, and dancing.

"Alas!" cried Queen Blanche, "the Fairy made me but a sad gift when she gave me a crown! People do not find happiness in magnificent palaces, but in the simple joys and labour of the country!"

As she finished speaking, the Fairy herself appeared before her.

"I did not intent to reward you by making you a Queen," she said, "but to punish you because you gave your plums with such bad grace. In order to be truly happy it is necessary to possess, like your sister, only those things that are simple and joyful, and not to wish for more."

"Ah, madame!" cried Blanche, "you are sufficiently avenged! Pray put an end to my misery!"

"It is ended," replied the Fairy. "Even now the King, who has ceased to love you, is sending his officers to forbid your returning to the palace."

All happened as the Fairy had said. And Blanche passed the rest of her life with Rose. She was happy and contented, never even thinking of the royal Court, except when she thanked the Fairy for taking her from it, and bringing her back to the pretty farm and to her dear sister.

THE ENCHANTED WATCH

Jean Macé (Adapted)

There once lived a gay young girl named Fannie, who never knew what time it was. Did she care? That I cannot say. And it is impossible for me to tell you how often she kept her father waiting, and caused him to be late for his appointments. And such a kind father as he was to Fannie, for she was his only child and he loved her very much. Indeed, he loved her so much that he overlooked her faults when he should have reproved them. Whole half-hours she used to keep the carriage waiting in front of the door, while she prinked before her mirror. And because she was never prompt, every one called her "Miss Tardy." Yet, after keeping people waiting, she would excuse herself in the sweetest manner possible, and blame herself for thoughtlessness.

One day her old Godmother wrote that she was coming the next morning to lunch with Fannie at noon. She was a Fairy so celebrated for her promptness that people called her "the Fairy Prompt," of which name she was very proud. With her, *noon* was not ten minutes after twelve, nor ten minutes before twelve, but it was *exactly twelve o'clock.*

So the next morning, at the first stroke of twelve, she set her foot on the bottom step of Fannie's house, and, as the last stroke died away, she entered the dining-room. The table was beautifully laid, and all was ready, but Fannie was not there. Indeed, Miss Tardy had forgotten all about her Godmother, and was calling on a friend. She was trying on her friend's beautiful new clothes and having such a fine time that the Godmother was utterly forgotten, as if she had never been in the world.

But at last hunger reminded Fannie of luncheon, and she hurried home. The servants informed her that her Godmother had arrived, but as Fannie's shoes pinched her, she rushed to her room and put on a pretty little pair of slippers. Then, as her street clothes were not suitable for slippers, she changed her

128

dress for a becoming house-gown. By this time it was two o'clock.

She found her Godmother asleep in a comfortable chair, such as is not made any more; and, I think, she was snoring a little. She awoke as Fannie opened the door hurriedly.

"My dear Godmother," said she, "I am so sorry!—so ashamed!—I am indeed a thoughtless creature to keep you waiting this way!"

"That is all right," said the Godmother, who was very kind and indulgent to Fannie. "I have slept a little, while waiting for you. That will do me no harm. What time is it?"

"Oh, please do not ask me!" begged Fannie, "you will make me die with shame!"

And like a playful child she ran and stood in front of the clock, but her Fairy Godmother, who had good eyes, saw that the hand had passed two o'clock.

The dinner, as you may well imagine, was overdone, but the Fairy, who really loved her goddaughter, took it all as good-naturedly as possible, and made many gay jokes as she tried to eat the burnt roasts and the scorched creams.

It was soon four o'clock, and Fannie's father hurriedly entered the drawing-room, where she was chatting with her Godmother.

"Well, Fannie!" he cried. "Are you ready? Are you ready?" Then he started back when he saw his daughter, in her pretty pink and blue house-gown, stretched indolently on a sofa, her feet to the fire, while she daintily sipped her coffee.

"What!" exclaimed her father. "Have you forgotten that you were to be ready at four o'clock!"

"Do you not see my Godmother with me, Papa?" said Fannie reproachfully.

"Pardon me, madame," said the father, turning to the Fairy and bowing, although his face was red with anger. "Excuse my rudeness, but my daughter will cause me to die with grief!"

"And what has the poor child done?" asked the Godmother.

"Judge for yourself," said he. "Prince Pandolph has invited us to his villa. Fannie is to sing for his guests. They are all assembled and expecting her. The Prince has sent his carriage which is now waiting before the door."

"But, Papa," said Fannie, "cannot you go without me?"

"You know that cannot be, child," said her father sadly. "It is you who are invited, and it is your fine voice that the Prince wishes for his musicale. He will now be offended for ever, since you cannot go in this dress."

"Calm yourself, my good sir," said the Godmother, seeing Fannie's confusion. "It is because of me that this dear little one has forgotten you. It is for me to repair this evil."

So saying she passed her hand over the unfortunate house-gown and it was instantly transformed into the most ravishing robe embroidered with gold and pearls. Fannie, who was naturally very pretty, shone like a star in this brilliant costume.

"Wait a minute," said the Fairy to the impatient father, who was already leading his daughter away. "Let me finish my work." And she put around the neck of her goddaughter a magnificent golden chain at the end of which hung an exquisite little watch the size of a locket, and all of chased gold studded with diamonds.

"Now, little one," said she, kissing the forehead of the spoilt child, "here is something that will aid your naughty memory. With this you will never again forget an engagement. Be sure to come home by ten o'clock."

"Oh, yes, indeed!" said Fannie, kissing her Godmother joyfully.

It is necessary to say here that it was the Fairy Prompt who invented watches in her youth. But hers were not like those sold nowadays in the shops. There was a magic virtue in each watch, for when the hour of an engagement arrived, it made so loud a ticking that the owner of it had no peace until he kept his engagement.

So it happened that while Fannie was listening to the praises of the Prince and his guests, who were saying that she had the most delightful voice in the world, she heard a gentle sound, but very distinct:—

"*Tic! Tic! Tic!*"

"It is ten o'clock!" exclaimed Fannie joyously to her father. "Oh! my dear, good, little watch, that my Godmother gave me, it has told me so! We must hurry home."

Her father, who was very much pleased because she had

charmed the Prince and his guests with her sweet voice, said as they drove away:—

"My dear child, to-morrow I am going to take you to the finest jeweller in town, and buy for you the bracelet of antique cameos that you have been begging me for. At what time do you wish to go? At ten o'clock?"

"Oh, no!" cried Fannie, her eyes sparkling with delight, "at nine o'clock, please! Ever since I saw the bracelet I have been dying to possess it!"

"Very good! At nine o'clock, then. And what shall we do with the rest of our morning?"

"At exactly ten I am to go to the dressmaker's to order some new gowns," said Fannie, "but may we not lunch together at eleven?"

"Just as you say, dear little nightingale," answered her father affectionately. "And order all the gowns and furbelows you wish, for the plumage should match the warbling. And since it suits you, I will meet you promptly at eleven, for at twelve I have an important business engagement."

"At eleven o'clock, then, dear Papa," said Fannie, "but do not forget to return in time this evening to escort me to the Baron's ball!"

"Don't worry!" said her father, smiling, "for nothing in the world would I make a pearl of a daughter like you wait for an escort!"

The next morning Fannie rose early and dressed more rapidly than usual, and was ready waiting for her father at nine. They drove to the jeweller's. How her eyes sparkled as her father clasped the cameo bracelet on her arm! But the jeweller, who hoped to sell Fannie a necklace as well, took from his showcase such beautiful collars of pearls, rubies, amethysts, and other gems and precious stones that she forgot how the time was flying.

"*Tic! Tic! Tic! Tic!*"

"Thank you, dear watch, for warning me!" said Fannie gaily, "but the dressmaker must wait!"

"*Tic! Tic! Tic! Tic! Tic!*"

"You insupportable thing!" cried she, and taking the watch from her neck she handed it to her father, saying: "I beg you, dear Papa, to put this in your pocket. It is very annoying!"

He took the watch, and seeing a friend on the street, went to the door to speak with him.

"*Toc! Toc! Toc! Toc!*"

The watch raised its voice so that Fannie should hear it. The people in the shop all asked where the noise came from. And her father, mortified, said good-bye to his friend, gave back the watch to Fannie, and hurried her into the carriage.

She was soon at the dressmaker's, and her ill-humour passed as she ordered a dress of pink brocade trimmed with rich lace, and a robe of garnet velvet embroidered with gold threads, and a cloak of silver cloth trimmed with pearls. She was not yet through when she glanced at the clock, and saw that it was eleven.

"Oh!" thought she, "that horrid watch is going to disturb me again! But I'll finish my ordering!"

"*Toc! Toc! Toc! Toc!*"

The dressmaker turned her head. "What's that, Miss?" she exclaimed with fright.

"It is nothing, let us go on!" said Miss Tardy.

"*Toc! Toc! Toc! Toc!*" louder than before.

"It is thieves! It is thieves!" cried the dressmaker.

"It is nothing I tell you—unfold this gown."

"*Toc!—Toc!—Toc!—Toc!*" louder and louder!

And the poor dressmaker, half dead with fright, was in such a state that she could show no more clothes. And Fannie put on her hat and coat, and hurried away to the restaurant where she found her father walking nervously up and down.

"Ah! how thoughtful of you, dear child, to be prompt!" he said, as he led her to a table. And the delicious food soon made her forget her annoyance.

When Fannie returned home she was so fatigued that she put on a charming wrapper, and lay down to rest. Then she remembered that she had an engagement to see a poor man at two o'clock, whose want she had promised to relieve. She took the fatal watch from her neck, and giving it to the maid, said:—

"Take this, and carry it to the cellar, so that I may be rid of it!"

Two o'clock struck, and the poor old man, who had had nothing to eat for three days, presented himself. The maid told him that Miss Fannie was sleeping and would not see him. With tears streaming down his cheeks, he bowed humbly and was turning away, when everybody in the house jumped to the ceiling.

"*Paf! Paf! Paf! Paf!*" It was like so many shots from a pistol.

The neighbours commenced screaming. The servants ran frantically to and fro.

Fannie sprang up from her couch.

"*Paf! Paf! Paf! Paf!*"

"It must be that wretched watch!" cried she.

"*Paf!—Paf!—Paf!—Paf!*"

"Yes! Yes! I am coming! I am coming!" And she hurried to the cellar and, picking up the watch, returned to her room in silence.

Then she called the poor old man, fed him, and comforted him, and sent him away with a full purse.

Evening arrived, and Fannie, all dressed for the Baron's ball, shone more beautifully than ever in her magnificent gown. And just as her father was leading her to the carriage, a clumsy wagon drove up, and an old countrywoman descended from it, crying out that she must see her dear child—her Fannie—just once more before she died. It was Fannie's old nurse who had come all the way from her village miles distant to hold her dear child in her arms. When she saw that Fannie was ready to go out, she screamed loudly and would have made herself ill, if Fannie had not embraced her tenderly, and promised to return before midnight. On the strength of this promise the old woman grew calm, and Fannie and her father went away to the ball.

But as the carriage drove through the streets, Fannie regretted her promise, and slipping her little hand under her cloak, she loosened the fatal watch, and flung it into a deep ditch.

"At last! At last!" she said to herself, with a sigh of relief.

Midnight sounded, and found her breathlessly twirling around in the dance, her eyes sparkling and her cheeks glowing.

"*Boom! Boom! Boom! Boom!*"

The orchestra stopped suddenly. The thunderclaps—for so they seemed to be—continued to follow each other without interruption.

"*Boom! Boom! Boom! Boom!*"

All the city was awake. Women cried out that the end of the world was come.

The unfortunate Fannie knew in a minute what it was. Fright seized her, and she lost her head. Instead of returning home quietly, which would have put an end to the horrible racket, she ran out into the street, and, wild with fright, hastened with all speed to the spot where she had thrown the watch.

"*Boom! Boom! Boom! Boom! Boom! Boom! Boom! Boom!*"

The houses were lighted. The amazed people thrust their heads out of the windows. All that they saw was a young girl running through the streets, her neck and head bare, and her ball-gown flying in the wind.

"*Boom! Boom! Boom! Boom! Boom! Boom! Boom! Boom!*"— every stroke was louder and more fearful.

The firemen came hurrying up to see if there was a fire, and one of them held his lantern under Fannie's nose, and cried out: "Why, it is little Miss Tardy! She has doubtless lost the time, and is hunting for it! Ha! Ha!"

Meanwhile Fannie ran on, and arrived breathlessly at the ditch into which she had flung the watch. Guided by its thunderous blows, she quickly laid her fingers on it. In a fury she was about to dash it against a stone when she felt a hand on her arm.

It was her Fairy Godmother, who, in gentle tones of reproach, said: "What are you doing, my child? You can never succeed!"

Then she took the watch from Fannie, which instantly became quiet, and passed the chain around the neck of her god-daughter, who was trembling with penitence and shame.

"Neither violence nor trickery," said her Godmother, "have any power over my gift to you. All you can do is to take it, and obey. And then you will find yourself happy."

At the same moment Miss Tardy felt herself being transported through the air, and found herself once more in her own room, holding the hand of her old nurse, who was weeping with tenderness and joy.

I have no need to tell you that Fannie never again attempted to disobey the protecting tyrant that she wore around her neck. And as the watch no longer had to warn her with its loud ticking, she learned in time to enjoy sacrificing her whims to her duty.

X. *Fairy Adventures*

BUTTERFLY'S DIAMOND

Lydia Maria Child (Adapted)

Once upon a time there was a little Fairy who was remarkable for her impatience and laziness. She was called Fairy Butterfly because she had such splendid green wings with silver spots on them. She loved dearly to be dressed in gorgeous colours, and to sleep in the rich chambers of the Foxgloves, or to flutter over beds of fragrant Mignonette. In truth, she was as luxurious a little Fairy as the sun ever shone on. So much did she like her ease that she would not gather a single dew-drop to bathe her face, nor would she pick a fresh rose-petal for a napkin. She played all day long, or slept curled up in the heart of a flower. Oh, she was a lazy Fairy!

When the Queen of the Fairies observed the faults of Butterfly, she resolved to help her to correct them. One day she summoned the lazy one to Court, and said:—

"Fairy Butterfly, we command you to go at once to the Green Cavern in the Island of Ceylon, and remain there until you have fashioned a diamond more pure and brilliant than any that has ever rested on the brow of mortal or Elf."

Little Butterfly bowed in silence and withdrew. As soon as she was outside the green mound in which the Fairy Queen held her Court, she burst into a passionate flood of tears.

"I shall have to watch that diamond for months and months and years and years," sobbed she, "and every day I must turn it over with my wand so that the crystals will form evenly! Oh, it is an endless labour to make a diamond! Oh, I am a most wretched Fairy!"

So she sat, and sobbed, and murmured for several minutes. Then she jumped up and stamped her little feet on the ground so furiously that the blue-eyed grasses trembled.

"I won't bear it!" she exclaimed. "I'll run away to the Fairies of the Air. I am sure they will be so pleased with my beauty that they will feed me, and I shall never need to work again! As for the diamond, why, it is just impossible for a little Fairy like me to make it!"

Then she peeped into a fountain to admire herself, and saw, alas! that the splendid green of her wings had faded, and the silver spots were dim. For, if Fairies have naughty thoughts, their wings always droop and their beauty fades. At this sight, little Butterfly wept aloud with vexation and shame.

"I suppose the old tyrant, our Queen, thinks that now I am so ugly, I'll hide myself in the Green Cavern in the Island of Ceylon! But I'll let her see that I do not care about her!" And, alas! as Butterfly spoke thus, the silver spots disappeared entirely, and her wings became a dirty brown.

Trembling with anger, the little one waved her wand, and called:—

> *"Hummingbird! Hummingbird!*
> *Come nigh! Come nigh!*
> *And carry me off*
> *To the far Blue Sky!"*

In an instant a tiny hummingbird, shining like a jewel, alighted at her feet. She sprang on his back, and away they flew to the golden clouds in the West where the Queen of the Air Fairies held her Court. And when the Queen and all her Fairies saw Butterfly's dirty brown wings, they waved their wands and vanished. And little Butterfly was left alone in the Palace of the Air.

But such a beautiful palace as it was! The clouds hung around it like transparent curtains of opal. The floor was paved with a rainbow. Thousands of gorgeous birds fluttered in the sunlight, and a multitude of voices filled the place with sweet sounds. Butterfly, fatigued by her flight through the sky and lulled by the voices, lay down on a rosy cloud, and fell into a gentle slumber.

When she awoke, she saw that a tiny bird, smaller than the hummingbird, was building a nest beside her. Straw after straw, shred after shred, the patient little creature brought in her bill and wove together. And then she flew away over hills and fields to find soft down with which to line the nest.

"She is a foolish thing!" murmured Butterfly. "How hard she works, and I don't believe that she will finish it after all!"

But soon the bird came back with her bill full of down, and lined the soft warm nest so that it was fit for a Fairy to sleep in. Butterfly peeped into it, and exclaimed, "Oh, what a pretty thing!"

Immediately she heard the tinkling of a lute, and a clear voice singing:—

"Bit by bit the bird builds her nest!"

She started up, and the Queen of the Air Fairies stood before her, clad in a robe of azure gossamer, embroidered with rainbow lights.

"Foolish Butterfly," said she, "we allow no idlers here. Obey your Queen, and go at once to the Green Cavern in the Island of Ceylon. Time and patience will accomplish all things. Go and make your diamond, and then you shall be welcome here." Butterfly tried to tell her how very hard it was to make a diamond, but the Queen of the Air Fairies flew away, touching her lute, and singing:—

"Bit by bit the bird builds her nest!"

Butterfly leaned her head upon her hands for a minute. She began to be ashamed of being so lazy, but she did not yet wish to go to the lonely Green Cavern, and work hard. So she waved her wand, and called again:—

"Hummingbird! Hummingbird!
Come nigh! Come nigh!
And carry me back
Through the clear Blue Sky!"

Immediately the little hummingbird returned, and she sprang on his back. He flew down with her, and she alighted near the green mound inside of which the Fairy Queen held her Court.

Close by the mound Butterfly saw some bees working in a crystal hive. Wearily and sadly she watched them. They left the hive, dipped into flowers, and carried their loads of sweet pollen back to the hive, and there they built their wax combs filled with golden honey. "I wish," thought she, "that I loved to work as hard as the bees do! But as for that diamond, it is useless to think about it! I should never finish it!"

Just then she heard strains of delightful music coming from the mound, and a chorus of Fairy voices singing:—

> *"Little by little the bee builds its cell!"*

Butterfly could have wept when she heard those familiar voices, for she longed to be with her Fairy sisters dancing hand-in-hand. "I will make the diamond," murmured she. "I shall surely get it done sometime! And I can fly home every night and dance in the Fairy Ring, or sleep in the flowers!"

Immediately a joyful strain of music rose on the air, and she heard her sisters' voices singing:—

> *"To the Green Cavern haste away!*
> *Sleep by night, and work by day!*
> *Little by little the gem will grow,*
> *Till pure as sunshine it will glow!"*

Alas! when Butterfly heard this, instead of flying at once to the Green Cavern, she began to think how hard she should have to work, and how many times she must turn the diamond. "I never can do it!" thought she. "I will go to the Queen of the Ocean Fairies. I am sure she will let me live in her Sea-Palace; and I need never work again!"

Mournful notes came from the mound, as Butterfly turned toward the seashore. When she reached the beach, she waved her wand, and called:—

> *"Nautilus! Nautilus!*
> *Come to me*
> *And carry me through*
> *The cold green Sea!"*

Immediately the delicate pearly boat of the nautilus came floating over the Ocean, and a wave landed it at Butterfly's feet. She stepped in, and down, down, under the waves she went, down to the bed of the Ocean, to a coral grove. And there was the magnificent palace of the Queen of the Ocean Fairies. Its pink coral pillars were twisted into a thousand beautiful forms. Pearls hung in deep festoons from the arches. The fan-coral and the sea-moss were formed into deep, cool bowers. And the hard, sandy floor was covered with many-coloured shells.

But as it had been in the Air, so it was in the Sea! When the Queen of the Ocean Fairies saw Butterfly's dirty brown wings, she and all her Court waved their wands and disappeared. And Butterfly was left alone in the Sea-Palace.

"How beautiful it is!" cried she. "Giants must have made these coral pillars!" As she spoke her eyes were nearly blinded by a swarm of tiny insects, and she saw them rest on an unfinished coral pillar. While she looked and wondered, she heard a thousand shell-trumpets being blown, and many voices singing:—

"Mite by mite the insect builds the coral bower!"

The sounds drew nearer and nearer, and a hundred Fairies, standing in beautiful shells, came floating through the water. In the largest shell of all was their Queen in a robe of wave-coloured silk spun by the Ocean silkworm. It was as thin as a spider's web, and the border was gracefully wrought with seed pearls.

"Foolish Butterfly," said the Queen, "learn to be industrious. We allow no idlers at our Court. Look at the coral pillars of my palace. They were made by these swarms of little creatures. Labour and patience did it all."

And she waved her wand, and the hundred shells floated away, while all the Fairies sang:—

"Mite by mite the insect builds the coral bower!"

"Well!" said Butterfly, sighing. "All creatures are busy, on the earth, in the air, and under the water. All things seem happy at their work. Perhaps I can learn to be so, too. I will make the diamond. And it shall be as pure and brilliant as a sunbeam in a water-drop!"

So Butterfly sought the Green Cavern in the Island of Ceylon. Day by day she worked as busily as the coral insects. She grew cheerful and happy. Her wings once more became a splendid green, and the silver spots were so bright that they seemed like sparks of fire. Never had she been so beautiful, never so much loved by the little birds and flowers.

After seven years had passed by, Butterfly knelt at the feet of her Queen and offered her diamond. It gave light like a star, and the whole Fairy Mound shone with its rays. And to this day the Fairies call it "Butterfly's Diamond."

LITTLE NIEBLA

W. H. Hudson (Condensed)

Have you seen the white mist over the River Yi in the morning—a light white mist that flies away when the sun gets hot? Yes? Then I will tell you a story about the white mist and a little girl named Alma.

Little Alma lived close to the River Yi, but far, far from here, beyond the trees and beyond the blue hills, for the Yi is a very long river. She lived with her grandmother and with six uncles, all big, tall men with long beards, and they always talked about wars, and cattle, and a great many other important things that Alma could not understand. There was no one to talk to Alma and for Alma to talk to or to play with. And when she went out of the house where all the big people were talking, she heard the cocks crowing, the dogs barking, the birds singing, the sheep bleating, and the trees rustling their leaves over her head, and she could not understand one word of all they said. At last, having no one to play with or talk to, she sat down and began to cry.

Now, it happened that near the spot where she sat there was an old black woman wearing a red shawl, who was gathering sticks for the fire, and she asked Alma why she cried.

"Because I have no one to talk to and play with," said Alma.

Then the old black woman drew a long brass pin out of her shawl, and pricked Alma's tongue with it, for she made Alma hold it out to be pricked.

"Now," said the old woman, "you can go and play and talk with the dogs, cats, birds, and trees, for you will understand all they say, and they will understand all you say."

Alma was very glad, and ran home as fast as she could to talk to the cat.

"Come, cat, let us talk and play together," she said.

141

"Oh, no," said the cat. "I am very busy watching a little bird, so you must go away and play with little Niebla down by the river."

Then the cat ran away among the weeds and left her. The dogs also refused to play when she went to them, for they had to watch the house and bark at strangers. Then they also told her to go and play with little Niebla down by the river.

Then Alma ran out, and caught a little duckling, a soft little thing, that looked like a ball of yellow cotton, and said: "Now, little duck, let us talk and play."

But the duckling only struggled to get away, and screamed: "Oh, Mamma! Mamma! Come and take me away from Alma!"

Then the old duck came rushing up, and said: "Alma, let my child alone; and if you want to play, go and play with Niebla down by the river. A nice thing to catch my duckie in your hands—what next, I wonder!"

So she let the duckling go, and at last she said, "Yes, I will go and play with Niebla down by the river."

She waited till she saw the white mist, and then ran all the way to the Yi, and stood still on the green bank close by the water with the white mist all round her.

By and by she saw a beautiful little child come flying toward her in the white mist. The child came and stood on the green bank, and looked at Alma. Very, very pretty she was; and she wore a white dress—whiter than milk, whiter than foam, and all embroidered with purple flowers. She had also white silk stockings and scarlet shoes, bright as scarlet verbenas. Her hair was long and fluffy, and shone like gold, and round her neck she had a string of big, gold beads.

Then Alma said, "Oh, beautiful little girl, what is your name?"

To which the little girl answered: "Niebla."

"Will you talk to me, and play with me?" said Alma.

"Oh, no," said Niebla; "how can I play with a little girl dressed as you are, and with bare feet?"

For, you know, poor Alma only wore a little old frock that came down to her knees, and she had no shoes and stockings on.

Then little Niebla rose up and floated away, away from the bank and down the river. And at last, when she was quite out of sight in the white mist, Alma began to cry. When it got very hot, she went and sat down, still crying, under the trees. There were two very big willow trees growing near the river. By and by the leaves rustled in the wind, and the trees began talking to each other, and Alma understood everything they said.

"Have you got any nests in your branches?" said one tree.

"Yes, one," said the other tree. "It was made by a little yellow bird, and there are five speckled eggs in it."

Then the first tree said: "There is little Alma sitting in our shade. Do you know why she is crying, Neighbour?"

The other tree answered: "Yes, it is because she has no one to play with. Little Niebla by the river refused to play with her because she is not beautifully dressed."

Then the first tree said: "Ah, she ought to go and ask the fox for some pretty clothes to wear. The fox always keeps a great store of pretty things in her hole."

Alma had listened to every word of this conversation. She remembered that a fox lived on the hillside not far off; for she had often seen it sitting in the sunshine, with its little ones playing round it and pulling their mother's tail in fun.

So Alma got up, and ran till she found the hole, and putting her head down it, she cried out: "Fox! Fox!"

But the fox seemed cross, and only answered, without coming out, "Go away, Alma, and talk to little Niebla. I am busy getting dinner for my children, and have no time to talk to you now."

Then Alma cried: "Oh, Fox, Niebla will not play with me because I have no pretty things to wear! Oh, Fox, will you give me a nice dress, and shoes and stockings, and a string of beads?"

After a little while the fox came out of its hole with a big bundle done up in a red cotton handkerchief, and said: "Here are the things, Alma, and I hope they will fit you. But, you know, Alma, you really ought not to come at this time of day, for I am very busy just now cooking the dinner—an armadillo roasted and a couple of partridges stewed with rice, and a little omelette of turkeys' eggs— I mean plovers' eggs, of course; I never touch turkeys' eggs."

Alma said she was very sorry to give so much trouble.

"Oh, never mind," said the fox. "How is your grandmother?"

"She is very well, thank you," said Alma, "but she has a bad headache."

"I am very sorry to hear it," said the fox. "Tell her to stick two fresh dock-leaves on her temples, and on no account to go out in the hot sun. Give her my best respects. And now, run home, Alma, and try on the things, and when you are passing this way, you can bring me back the handkerchief, as I always tie my face up in it when I have the toothache."

Alma thanked the fox very much, and ran home as fast as she could; and when the bundle was opened she found in it a beautiful white dress embroidered with purple flowers, a pair of scarlet shoes, silk stockings, and a string of great golden beads.

They all fitted her very well; and next day, when the white mist was on the Yi, she dressed herself in her beautiful clothes, and went down to the river. By and by little Niebla came flying along; and when she saw Alma, she came and kissed her, and took her by the hand. All the morning they played and talked together, gathering flowers and running races over the green sward. And, at last, Niebla bade her good-bye, and flew away, for all the white mist was floating off down the river.

But every day after that, Alma found her little companion by the Yi, and was very happy, for now she had some one to talk to and to play with.

LITTLE TINY

Hans Christian Andersen

There was once a woman who wished very much to have a little child; so she went to a Fairy, and said: "I should so very much like to have a little child. Can you tell me where I may find one?"

"Oh, that is easily managed," said the Fairy. "Here is a barley-corn of a different kind to those which grow in the farmers' fields, and which the chickens eat. Put it into a flower-pot, and see what will happen."

"Thank you," said the woman, and she gave the Fairy twelve shillings, which was the price of the barley-corn. Then she went home and planted it, and immediately there grew up a large handsome flower, something like a tulip in appearance, but with its leaves tightly closed as if it was still a bud.

"It is a beautiful flower," said the woman, and she kissed the red and golden-coloured leaves, and while she did so the flower opened, and she could see that it was a real tulip.

Within the flower, upon the green velvet stamens, sat a very delicate and graceful little maiden. She was scarcely half as long as a thumb, and they gave her the name of "Little Thumb," or Tiny, because she was so small. A walnut-shell, elegantly polished, served her for a cradle. Her bed was formed of blue violet-leaves, with a rose-leaf for a counterpane.

Here she slept at night, but during the day she amused herself on a table, where the woman had placed a plateful of water. Round this plate were wreaths of flowers with their stems in the water, and upon it floated a large tulip-leaf, which served Tiny for a boat. Here the little maiden sat and rowed herself from side to side, with two oars made of white horse-hair. It really was a very pretty sight. Tiny could, also, sing so softly and sweetly that nothing like her singing had ever before been heard.

One night, while she lay in her pretty bed, a large, ugly, wet

145

toad crept through a broken pane of glass in the window, and leaped right up on the table where Tiny lay sleeping under her rose-leaf quilt.

"What a pretty little wife this would make for my son!" said the toad, and she took up the walnut-shell in which little Tiny lay asleep, and jumped through the window with it into the garden.

In the swampy margin of a broad stream in the garden lived the toad, with her son. He was uglier even than his mother, and when he saw the pretty little maiden in her elegant bed, he could only cry: "*Croak, croak, croak.*"

"Don't speak so loud, or she will wake," said the toad, "and then she might run away, for she is as light as swan's down. We will place her on one of the water-lily leaves out in the stream. It will be like an island to her, she is so light and small, and then she cannot escape. And, while she is away, we will make haste and prepare the state-room under the marsh, in which you are to live when you are married."

Far out in the stream grew a number of water-lilies, with broad green leaves, which seemed to float on the top of the water. The largest of these leaves appeared farther off than the rest, and the old toad swam out to it with the walnut-shell, in which little Tiny lay still asleep.

The little creature woke very early in the morning, and began to cry bitterly when she found where she was, for she could see nothing but water on every side of the large green leaf, and no way of reaching the land.

Meanwhile the old toad was very busy under the marsh, decking her room with rushes and wild yellow flowers, to make it look pretty for her new daughter-in-law. Then she swam out with her ugly son to the leaf on which she had placed poor little Tiny. She wanted to fetch the pretty bed, that she might put it in the bridal chamber to be ready for her.

The old toad bowed low to her in the water, and said: "Here is my son. He will be your husband, and you will live happily together in the marsh by the stream."

"*Croak, croak, croak,*" was all her son could say for himself. So the toad took up the elegant little bed, and swam away with it, leaving Tiny all alone on the green leaf, where she sat and

wept. She could not bear to think of living with the old toad, and
having her ugly son for a husband.

The little fishes, who swam about in the water, had seen the
toad, and heard what she said, so they lifted their heads above
the water to look at the little maiden. As soon as they caught
sight of her, they saw she was very pretty, and it made them
sorry to think that she must go and live with the ugly toads. "No,
it must never be!" so they assembled together in the water,
round the green stalk which held the leaf on which the little
maiden stood, and gnawed it away at the root with their teeth.
Then the leaf floated down the stream, carrying Tiny far away.

Tiny sailed past many towns, and the little birds in the bushes
saw her, and sang: "What a lovely little creature!" So the leaf
swam away with her farther and farther, till it brought her to
other lands. A graceful little white butterfly constantly fluttered
round her, and at last alighted on the leaf. Tiny pleased him, and
she was glad of it, for now the toad could not possibly reach her,
and the country through which she sailed was beautiful, and the
sun shone upon the water, till it glittered like liquid gold. She
took off her girdle and tied one end of it round the butterfly, and
the other end of the ribbon she fastened to the leaf, which now
glided on much faster than ever, taking little Tiny with it as
she stood.

Presently a large cockchafer flew by. The moment he caught
sight of her, he seized her round her delicate waist with his
claws, and flew with her into a tree. The green leaf floated away
on the brook, and the butterfly flew with it, for he was fastened
to it, and could not get away.

Oh, how frightened little Tiny felt when the cockchafer flew
with her to the tree! But especially was she sorry for the beautiful white butterfly which she had fastened to the leaf, for if he
could not free himself he would die of hunger. But the
cockchafer did not trouble himself at all about the matter. He
seated himself by her side on a large green leaf, gave her some
honey from the flowers to eat, and told her she was very pretty,
though not in the least like a cockchafer. After a time, all the
cockchafers who lived in the tree came to visit her. They stared
at Tiny, and then the young lady-cockchafers turned up their

feelers, and said: "She has only two legs! how ugly that looks."
"She has no feelers," said another. "Her waist is quite slim.
Pooh! she is like a human being."

"Oh! she is ugly!" said all the lady-cockchafers, although Tiny
was very pretty. Then the cockchafer who had run away with
her, believed all the others when they said she was ugly, and
would have nothing more to say to her, and told her she might
go where she liked. Then he flew down with her from the tree,
and placed her on a daisy, and she wept at the thought that she
was so ugly that even the cockchafers would have nothing to say
to her. And all the while she was really the loveliest creature that
one could imagine, and as tender and delicate as a beautiful
rose-leaf!

During the whole summer poor little Tiny lived quite alone in
the wide forest. She wove herself a bed with blades of grass, and
hung it up under a broad leaf, to protect herself from the rain.
She sucked the honey from the flowers for food, and drank the
dew from their leaves every morning. So passed away the
Summer and the Autumn, and then came the Winter,—the
long, cold Winter.

All the birds who had sung to her so sweetly were flown away,
and the trees and the flowers had withered. The large clover leaf
under the shelter of which she had lived, was now rolled
together and shrivelled up, nothing remained but a yellow withered stalk. She felt dreadfully cold, for her clothes were torn,
and she was herself so frail and delicate, that, poor little thing,
she was nearly frozen to death! It began to snow too; and the
snow-flakes, as they fell upon her, were like a whole shovelful
falling upon one of us, for we are tall, but she was only an inch
high. Then she wrapped herself up in a dry leaf, but it cracked
in the middle and could not keep her warm, and she shivered
with cold.

Near the wood in which she had been living lay a large corn-
field, but the corn had been cut a long time; nothing remained
but the bare dry stubble standing up out of the frozen ground.
It was to her like struggling through a large wood. Oh! how she
shivered with the cold. She came at last to the door of a field-
mouse, who had a little den under the corn-stubble. There

dwelt the field-mouse in warmth and comfort, with a whole roomful of corn, a kitchen, and a beautiful dining-room. Poor little Tiny stood before the door just like a little beggar-girl, and begged for a small piece of barley-corn, for she had been without a morsel to eat for two days.

"You poor little creature," said the field-mouse, who was really a good old field-mouse, "come into my warm room and dine with me." She was very pleased with Tiny, so she said: "You are quite welcome to stay with me all the Winter, if you like; but you must keep my rooms clean and neat, and tell me stories, for I shall like to hear them very much." And Tiny did all the field-mouse asked her, and found herself very comfortable.

"We shall have a visitor soon," said the field-mouse one day. "My neighbour pays me a visit once a week. He is better off than I am. He has large rooms, and wears a beautiful black velvet coat. If you could only have him for a husband, you would be well provided for indeed! But he is blind, so you must tell him some of your prettiest stories."

But Tiny did not feel at all interested about this neighbour, for he was a mole. However, he came and paid a visit, dressed in his black velvet coat.

"He is very rich and learned, and his house is twenty times larger than mine," said the field-mouse.

He was rich and learned, no doubt, but he always spoke slightingly of the sun and the pretty flowers, because he had never seen them. Tiny was obliged to sing to him: "Lady-bird, lady-bird, fly away home," and many other pretty songs. And the mole fell in love with her because she had such a sweet voice. But he said nothing yet, for he was very cautious.

A short time before, the mole had dug a long passage under the earth, which led from the dwelling of the field-mouse to his own, and here she had permission to walk with Tiny whenever she liked. But he warned them not to be alarmed at the sight of a dead bird which lay in the passage. It was a perfect bird, with a beak and feathers, and could not have been dead long, and was lying just where the mole had made his passage.

The mole took a piece of phosphorescent wood in his mouth, and it glittered like fire in the dark. Then he went before them

to light them through the long, dark passage. When they came
to the spot where lay the dead bird, the mole pushed his broad
nose through the ceiling, the earth gave way, so that there was a
large hole, and the daylight shone into the passage.

In the middle of the floor lay the dead swallow, his beautiful
wings pulled close to his sides, his feet and his head drawn up
under his feathers. The poor bird had evidently died of the cold.
It made little Tiny very sad to see it, she did so love the little
birds. All the Summer they had sung and twittered for her so
beautifully.

But the mole pushed it aside with his crooked legs, and said:
"He will sing no more now. How miserable it must be to be born
a little bird! I am thankful that none of my children will ever be
birds, for they can do nothing but cry, 'Tweet, tweet,' and always
die of hunger in the Winter."

"Yes, you may well say that, you clever man!" exclaimed the
field-mouse. "What is the use of his twittering, for when Winter
comes he must either starve or be frozen to death. Still, birds
are very high-bred."

Tiny said nothing; but when the others had turned their backs
on the bird, she stooped down and stroked aside the soft feathers which covered the head, and kissed the closed eyelids.
"Perhaps this was the one who sang to me so sweetly in the
Summer," she said; "and how much pleasure it gave me, you
dear, pretty bird."

The mole now stopped up the hole through which the daylight shone, and then accompanied Tiny and the field-mouse
home.

But during the night Tiny could not sleep; so she got out of
bed and wove a large, beautiful carpet of hay. Then she carried
it to the dead bird, and spread it over him, with some down from
the flowers which she had found in the field-mouse's room. The
down was as soft as wool, and she spread some of it on each side
of the bird, so that he might lie warmly in the cold earth.

"Farewell, you pretty little bird!" said she, "farewell! Thank
you for your delightful singing during the Summer, when all the
trees were green, and the warm sun shone upon us."

Then she laid her head on the bird's breast, but she was

alarmed immediately, for it seemed as if something inside the bird went *"thump, thump."* It was the bird's heart! He was not really dead, only benumbed with the cold, and the warmth had restored him to life. In Autumn all the swallows fly away into warm countries, but if one happens to linger, the cold seizes it, it becomes frozen, and falls down as if dead. It remains where it fell, and the cold snow covers it. Tiny trembled very much. She was quite frightened, for the bird was large, a great deal larger than herself—she was only an inch high. But she took courage, laid the wool more thickly over the poor swallow, and then took a leaf which she had used for her own counterpane, and laid it over the head of the poor bird.

The next morning she again stole out to see him. He was alive but very weak. He could only open his eyes for a moment to look at Tiny, who stood by holding a piece of decayed wood in her hand, for she had no other lantern.

"Thank you, pretty little maiden," said the sick swallow; "I have been so nicely warmed, that I shall soon regain my strength, and be able to fly about in the warm sunshine."

"Oh," said she, "it is cold out of doors now. It snows and freezes. Stay in your warm bed. I will take care of you."

Then she brought the swallow some water in a flower-leaf, and after he had drunk, he told her that he had wounded one of his wings in a thornbush, and could not fly so fast as the other birds, who were soon far away on their journey to warm countries. Then at last he had fallen to the earth, and could remember no more nor how he came to be where she had found him.

The whole Winter the swallow remained underground, and Tiny nursed him with care and love. Neither the mole nor the field-mouse knew anything about it, for they did not like swallows. Very soon the Spring-time came, and the sun warmed the earth. Then the swallow bade farewell to Tiny, and she opened the hole in the ceiling which the mole had made. The sun shone in upon them so beautifully that the swallow asked her if she would go with him. She could sit on his back, he said, and he would fly away with her into the green woods. But Tiny knew it would make the field-mouse very grieved if she left her in that manner, so she said: "No, I cannot."

"Farewell, then, farewell, you good, pretty, little maiden!" said the swallow. And he flew out into the sunshine.

Tiny looked after him, and the tears rose in her eyes. She was very fond of the poor swallow.

"Tweet! Tweet!" sang the bird, as he flew out into the green woods, and Tiny felt sad. She was not allowed to go out into the warm sunshine. The corn which had been sown in the field over the house of the field-mouse had grown up high into the air, and formed a thick wood to Tiny, who was only an inch high.

"You are going to be married, Tiny," said the field-mouse. "My neighbour has asked for you. What good fortune for a poor child like you! Now we will prepare your wedding clothes. They must be both woollen and linen. Nothing must be wanting when you are the mole's wife."

Tiny had to turn the spindle; and the field-mouse hired four spiders, who were to weave day and night. Every evening the mole visited her, and was continually speaking of the time when the Summer would be over. Then he would keep his wedding-day with Tiny. But now the heat of the sun was so great that it burned the earth, and made it quite hard, like a stone. As soon as the Summer was over, the wedding should take place.

But Tiny was not at all pleased; for she did not like the tiresome mole. Every morning when the sun rose, and every evening when it went down, she would creep out at the door, and as the wind blew aside the ears of corn, so that she could see the blue sky, she thought how beautiful and bright it seemed out there, and wished so much to see her dear swallow again. But he never returned; for by this time he had flown far away into the lovely green forest.

When Autumn arrived, Tiny had her outfit quite ready; and the field-mouse said to her: "In four weeks the wedding must take place."

Then Tiny wept, and said she would not marry the disagreeable mole.

"Nonsense," replied the field-mouse. "Now, don't be obstinate, or I shall bite you with my white teeth. He is a very handsome mole. The Queen herself does not wear more beautiful velvets and furs. His kitchen and cellars are quite full. You ought to be very thankful for such good fortune."

So the wedding-day was fixed, on which the mole was to fetch Tiny away to live with him, deep under the earth, and never again to see the warm sun, because *he* did not like it. The poor child was most unhappy at the thought of saying farewell to the beautiful sun; and, as the field-mouse had given her permission to stand at the door, she went to look at it once more.

"Farewell, bright sun!" she cried, stretching out her arm toward it. And then she walked a short distance from the house; for the corn had been cut, and only the dry stubble remained in the fields. "Farewell! Farewell!" she repeated, twining her arm round a little red flower that grew just by her side. "Greet the little swallow from me, if you should see him again."

"Tweet! Tweet!" sounded over her head suddenly. She looked up, and there was the swallow himself flying close by. As soon as he spied Tiny, he was delighted; and then she told him how unwilling she felt to marry the ugly mole, and to live always beneath the earth, and never to see the bright sun any more. And as she told him she wept.

"Cold Winter is coming," said the swallow, "and I am going to fly away into warmer countries. Will you go with me? You can sit on my back, and fasten yourself on with your sash. Then we can fly away from the ugly mole and his gloomy rooms—far away, over the mountains, into warmer countries, where the sun shines more brightly than here; where it is always Summer, and the flowers bloom in greater beauty. Fly now with me, dear little Tiny! You save my life when I lay frozen in that dark, dreary passage."

"Yes, I will go with you," said Tiny. And she seated herself on the bird's back, with her feet on his outstretched wings, and tied her girdle to one of his strongest feathers.

Then the swallow rose in the air, and flew over forest and over sea, high above the highest mountains, covered with eternal snow. Tiny would have been frozen in the cold air, but she crept under the bird's warm feathers, keeping her little head uncovered, so that she might admire the beautiful lands over which they passed.

At length they reached the warm countries, where the sun shines brightly, and the sky seems so much higher above the earth. Here, on the hedges, and by the wayside, grew purple, green, and white grapes; lemons and oranges hung from trees in the woods; and the air was fragrant with myrtles and orange blossoms. Beautiful children ran along the country lanes, playing with large gay butterflies. And, as the swallow flew farther and farther, every place appeared still more lovely.

At last they came to a blue lake, and by the side of it, shaded by trees of the deepest green, stood a palace of dazzling white marble, built in the olden times. Vines clustered round its lofty pillars, and at the top were many swallows' nests, and one of these was the home of the swallow who carried Tiny.

"This is my house," said the swallow; "but it would not do for you to live there—you would not be comfortable. You must choose for yourself one of those lovely flowers, and I will put you down upon it, and then you shall have everything that you can wish to make you happy."

"That will be delightful!" she said, and clapped her little hands for joy.

A large marble pillar lay on the ground, which, in falling, had been broken into three pieces. Between these pieces grew the most beautiful large white flowers; so the swallow flew down with Tiny, and placed her on one of the broad leaves. But how surprised she was to see, in the middle of the flowers, a tiny little man, as white and transparent as if he had been made of crystal! He had a gold crown on his head, and delicate wings at his shoulders, and was not much larger than Tiny herself. He was the Fairy of the flower; for a tiny man and a tiny woman dwell in every flower; and this was the King of them all.

"Oh, how beautiful he is!" whispered Tiny to the swallow.

The little King was at first quite frightened at the bird, who was like a giant compared to such a delicate little creature as himself. But when he saw Tiny, he was delighted, and thought her the prettiest little maiden he had ever seen. He took the gold crown from his head, and placed it on hers, and asked her name, and if she would be his wife, and Queen over all the flowers.

This certainly was a very different sort of husband to the son of the toad, or the mole, with his black velvet and fur; so she said "Yes," to the handsome King.

Then all the flowers opened, and out of each came a little lady or a tiny lord, all so pretty it was quite a pleasure to look at them. Each of them brought Tiny a present. But the best gift was a pair of beautiful wings, which had belonged to a large white fly, and they fastened them to Tiny's shoulders, so that she might fly from flower to flower.

Then there was much rejoicing, and the little swallow, who sat above them, in his nest, was asked to sing a wedding song, which he did as well as he could; but in his heart he felt sad, for he was very fond of Tiny, and would have liked never to part from her again.

"You must not be called Tiny any more," said the Fairy of the flowers to her. "It is an ugly name, and you are so very pretty. We will call you Maia."

"Farewell! Farewell!" said the swallow, with a heavy heart as he left the warm countries, to fly back into Denmark. There he had a nest over the window of a house in which dwelt the writer of Fairy tales. The swallow sang, "Tweet! Tweet!" And from his song came this whole story.

THE IMMORTAL FOUNTAIN

Lydia Maria Child (Adapted)

In ancient times two little Princesses lived in Scotland, one of whom was extremely beautiful, and the other dwarfish, dark-coloured, and deformed. One was named Rose, and the other Marion.

The sisters did not live happily together. Marion hated Rose because the latter was handsome and everybody praised her. So Marion scowled and her face grew absolutely black when anybody asked her how her pretty little sister was. And once she was so wicked and jealous that she cut off all Rose's glossy golden hair, and threw it in the fire. Poor Rose cried bitterly about it, but she did not scold or strike her sister, for she was an amiable and gentle little being.

No wonder, then, that all the family and all the neighbours disliked Marion; and no wonder that her face grew uglier and uglier every day. But the neighbours used to say that Rose had been blessed by the Fairies, to whom she owed her extraordinary beauty and goodness.

Not far from the castle where the Princesses resided was a deep grotto, said to lead to the Palace of Beauty where the Queen of the Fairies held her Court. Some said that Rose had fallen asleep there one day when she was tired of chasing a butterfly, and that the Queen had dipped her in an Immortal Fountain, from which she had risen with the beauty of an angel. Marion often asked Rose about this story, but the child always replied that she was forbidden to speak of it. When Rose saw any uncommon bird or butterfly, she would exclaim: "Oh, how much that looks like Fairyland!" But when asked what she knew about Fairyland, she blushed and would not answer.

Marion thought a great deal about this. "Why can I not go to the Palace of Beauty?" thought she. "And why may I not bathe in the Immortal Fountain?"

One Summer's noon, when all was still save the faint twitterings of birds and the lazy hum of bees, Marion entered the deep grotto. She sat down on a bank of moss. The air around her was as fragrant as if it came from a bed of violets. And with the far-off sound of music in her ears, she fell into a gentle slumber.

When she awoke it was evening, and she found herself in a small hall, where opal pillars supported a rainbow roof, the bright reflection of which rested on crystal walls and on a golden floor inlaid with pearls. All around, between the opal pillars, stood the tiniest vases of pure alabaster, in which grew a multitude of brilliant and fragrant flowers; some of which, twining around the pillars, were lost in the floating rainbow above. This scene of beauty was lighted by millions of fireflies glittering in the air like wandering stars.

While Marion was gazing in amazement at all this, a little lady of rare loveliness stood before her. Her robe was of green and gold. Her flowing gossamer mantle was caught upon one shoulder with a pearl, and in her hair was a solitary star composed of five diamonds, each no bigger than a pin point. She smiled at Marion and sang:—

> *"The Fairy Queen*
> *Hath rarely seen*
> *Creature of earthly mould*
> *Within her door*
> *On pearly floor*
> *Inlaid with shining gold!*
> *Mortal, all thou seest is fair!*
> *Quick! Thy purposes declare!"*

As she concluded, the song was taken up and thrice repeated by a multitude of soft voices in the distance. It seemed as if birds and insects joined in the chorus; and ever and anon between the pauses, the sound of a cascade was heard, whose waters fell in music.

All these delightful sounds died away, and the Queen of the Fairies stood patiently awaiting Marion's answer. Curtsying low, and with a trembling voice, the little maiden said:—

"Will it please Your Majesty to make me as handsome as my sister Rose?"

The Queen smiled again. "I will grant your request," said she, "if you will promise to fulfil all the conditions I propose."

Marion eagerly promised that she would.

"The Immortal Fountain," continued the Queen, "is on the top of a high, steep hill. At four different places Fairies are stationed around it, who guard it with their wands. None can pass except those who obey my orders. Go home now. For one week speak no ungentle word to your sister. At the end of that time come again to the grotto."

Marion went home light of heart. Rose was in the garden, watering flowers. And the first thing Marion observed was that her sister's sunny hair had grown as long and beautiful as before it was cut off. The sight made her angry, and she was just about to snatch the watering-pot from Rose's hand with cross words, when she remembered the Fairy, and passed into the castle in silence.

The end of the week arrived, and Marion had faithfully kept her promise. Again she entered the grotto. The Queen was feasting when Marion reached the hall with opal pillars. The bees had brought, as a gift, golden honey, and placed it on small rose-coloured shells which adorned a crystal table. Bright butterflies floated about the head of the Queen, and fanned her with their wings. Fireflies flew near to give her light. And a large diamond beetle formed her footstool. After she had supped, a dew-drop on a violet petal was brought her to bathe her royal fingers.

Behind the Queen's chair hovered numerous bright Fairies, but when Marion entered the diamond sparkles on their wings faded as they always do in the presence of anything bad. And in a second all the Queen's attendants vanished, singing as they went:—

> *"The Fairy Queen*
> *Hath rarely seen*
> *Creature of mortal mould*
> *Within her door*
> *On pearly floor*
> *Inlaid with shining gold!"*

"Mortal, have you fulfilled your promise?" asked the Queen.
"I have," replied the maiden.

"Then follow me."

Marion did as she was directed, and away they hastened over beds of Violets and Mignonette. Birds sang, butterflies fluttered, and the voices of many fountains came on the breeze.

Presently they reached the hill on the top of which was the Immortal Fountain. The foot of the hill was surrounded by a band of Fairies clothed in green gossamer, and with their ivory wands crossed to bar the ascent. The Queen waved her wand over them, and immediately they stretched their transparent wings and flew away.

The hill was steep, and far, far up climbed the Queen and Marion. The air became more and more fragrant; and more and more distinctly they heard the sound of waters falling in music. At length they were stopped by another band of Fairies, clothed in blue gossamer, with silver wands crossed.

"Here," said the Queen, "our journey must end. You can go no further until you have fulfilled the orders I shall give you. Go home now. For one month do by your sister as you would wish her to do by you, if you were Rose and she Marion."

Marion promised and departed. She found the task harder than the first had been. When Rose asked her for playthings, she found it hard to give them gently and affectionately. When Rose talked to her, she wanted to go away in silence. And when a pocket mirror was found in her sister's room, broken into a thousand pieces, she felt sorely tempted to conceal that she had done the mischief. But she was so anxious to be made beautiful that she did as she wished to be done by.

All the household remarked how Marion had changed.

"I love her dearly!" said Rose; "she is so good and amiable."

"So do I!" said a dozen voices.

Marion blushed deeply, and her eyes sparkled with pleasure. "How pleasant it is to be loved!" thought she.

At the end of the month she went to the grotto again. Again the Fairy Queen conducted her up the hill, and this time the Fairies in blue lowered their silver wands and flew away. The two travelled on, higher and higher. The path grew steeper and steeper, but the fragrant air became more delicious, and more distinctly was heard the sound of waters falling in music.

At length their course was stayed by a troop of Fairies clothed in rainbow robes, and holding silver wands tipped with gold. In face and form they were far more beautiful than anything Marion had yet seen.

"Here we must pause," said the Queen. "This boundary you cannot yet pass."

"Why not?" asked the impatient Marion.

"Because those who pass the Rainbow Fairies must be very pure," replied the Queen.

"Am I not very pure?" asked the maiden. "All the people in the castle tell me how good I have grown."

"Mortal eyes see only the outside," answered the Queen. "But those who pass the Rainbow Fairies must be pure in thought as well as action. Go home now. For three months never indulge in a wicked or envious thought. You shall then have a glimpse of the Immortal Fountain."

Marion returned home. At the end of three months she again visited the hall with opal pillars. The Queen did not smile when she saw her; but in silence led the way up the hill toward the Immortal Fountain. The Green Fairies and the Blue Fairies flew away as they approached; but the Rainbow Fairies bowed low to the Queen, and kept their gold-tipped wands firmly crossed.

Marion saw that the silver specks on the Fairies' wings began to grow dim, and she burst into tears.

"I knew," said the Queen, "that you could not pass this boundary. Envy has been in your heart. But be not discouraged, for years you have been indulging in wrong feelings; and you must not wonder if it takes many months to drive them out. Go home and try once more."

So poor Marion went sadly away. And when she visited the hall again, the Queen smiled, and touched her playfully with her wand. She then led her up the hill to the Immortal Fountain. The silver specks on the wings of the Rainbow Fairies shone bright as Marion approached, and the Fairies lowered their wings and flew away.

And now every footstep was on flowers that yielded beneath the feet like a pathway of clouds. The delicious fragrance could almost be felt, and loud and clear and sweet came the sound of waters falling in music. And now Marion could see a cascade leaping and sparkling over crystal rocks. Above it rested a rainbow. The spray fell in pearls forming delicate foliage around the margin of the Fountain. And deep and silent below the foam of the cascade was the Immortal Fountain of Beauty. Its amber-coloured waves flowed over a golden bed, and many Fairies were bathing in its waves, the diamonds in their hair gleaming like sunbeams on the water.

"Oh, let me bathe in the Fountain!" cried Marion, clapping her hands in delight.

"Not yet," said the Queen. "Behold the Purple Fairies with golden wands that guard its brink."

Marion looked, and saw Beings lovelier than any her eye had ever rested on.

"You cannot pass them yet," said the Queen. "Go home. For one year drive from your heart all evil feelings, not for the sake of bathing in this Fountain, but because goodness is lovely and desirable for its own sake. Then your work is done."

Marion returned home. This was the hardest task of all. For she had been willing to be good, not because it was right, but because she wished to be beautiful. Three times she sought the grotto, and three times she left in tears, for the golden specks on the wings of the Purple Fairies grew dim as she approached, and the golden wands were still crossed to shut her from the Immortal Fountain.

But the fourth time the Purple Fairies lowered their wands, singing:—

> *"Thou hast scaled the mountain,*
> *Go, bathe in the Fountain;*
> *Rise fair to the sight,*
> *As an angel of light;*
> *Go bathe in the Fountain!"*

Marion, full of joy, was about to plunge in, but the Queen touched her, saying:—

"Look in the mirror of the water. Art thou not already as beautiful as heart can wish?"

Marion looked at herself, and saw that her eyes sparkled with new lustre, a bright colour shone in her cheeks, her hair waved softly about her face, and dimples played sweetly around her mouth.

"But I have not touched the Immortal Fountain!" cried she, turning in surprise to the Queen.

"True," replied the Queen. "But its waters have been within your soul. Know that a pure and happy heart, and gentleness toward others, are the only Immortal Fountains of Beauty!"

Marion thanked the Queen, and joyfully returned home.

Rose ran to meet her, and clasped her to her bosom fervently.

"I know all," she said; "I have been in Fairyland. Disguised as a bird, I have watched all your steps. When you first went to the grotto, I begged the Queen to grant your wish."

Ever after the sisters lived lovingly together. It was the remark of every one: "How handsome Marion has grown! The ugly scowl has departed from her face, her eyes are so clear and gentle, her mouth is so pretty and smiling. To my taste she is as handsome as Rose."

THE STORY OF CHILDE CHARITY

Frances Browne

Once upon a time there lived in the west country a little girl who had neither father nor mother; they both died when she was very young, and left their daughter to the care of her uncle, who was the richest farmer in all that country. He had houses and lands, flocks and herds, many servants to work about his house and fields, a wife who had brought him a great dowry, and two fair daughters.

All their neighbours, being poor, looked up to the family—insomuch that they imagined themselves great people. The father and mother were as proud as peacocks; the daughters thought themselves the greatest beauties in the world, and not one of the family would speak civilly to anybody they thought low.

Now it happened that though she was their near relation, they had this opinion of the orphan girl, partly because she had no fortune, and partly because of her humble, kindly disposition. It was said that the more needy and despised any creature was, the more ready was she to befriend it: on which account the people of the west country called her Childe Charity, and if she had any other name, I never heard it.

Childe Charity was thought very mean in that proud house. Her uncle would not own her for his niece; her cousins would not keep her company; and her aunt sent her to work in the dairy, and to sleep in the back garret, where they kept all sorts of lumber and dry herbs for the winter. The servants learned the same tune, and Childe Charity had more work than rest among them. All the day she scoured pails, scrubbed dishes, and washed crockeryware. But every night she slept in the back garret as sound as a Princess could in her palace chamber.

Her uncle's house was large and white, and stood among green meadows by a river's side. In front it had a porch covered with a vine; behind, it had a farmyard and high granaries. Within, there were two parlours for the rich, and two kitchens for the poor, which the neighbours thought wonderfully grand. And one day in the harvest season, when this rich farmer's corn had been all cut down and housed, he condescended so far as to invite his neighbourhood to a harvest supper. The west country people came in their holiday clothes and best behaviour. Such heaps of cakes and cheese, such baskets of apples and barrels of ale, had never been at feast before.

They were making merry in kitchen and parlour, when a poor old woman came to the back door, begging for broken victuals and a night's lodging. Her clothes were coarse and ragged; her hair was scanty and grey; her back was bent; her teeth were gone. She had a squinting eye, a clubbed foot, and crooked fingers. In short, she was the poorest and ugliest old woman that ever came begging.

The first who saw her was the kitchen-maid, and she ordered her to be gone for an ugly witch. The next was the herd-boy, and he threw her a bone over his shoulder. But Childe Charity, hearing the noise, came out from her seat at the foot of the lowest table, and asked the old woman to take her share of the supper, and sleep that night in her bed in the back garret.

The old woman sat down without a word of thanks. All the company laughed at Childe Charity for giving her bed and her supper to a beggar. Her proud cousins said it was just like her mean spirit, but Childe Charity did not mind them. She scraped the pots for her supper that night and slept on a sack among the lumber, while the old woman rested in her warm bed.

And next morning, before the little girl awoke, the old woman was up and gone, without so much as saying "Thank you," or "Good morning."

That day all the servants were sick after the feast, and mostly cross too—so you may judge how civil they were; when, at supper time, who should come to the back door but the old woman, again asking for broken victuals and a night's lodging.

No one would listen to her or give her a morsel, till Childe Charity rose from her seat at the foot of the lowest table, and kindly asked her to take her supper, and sleep in her bed in the back garret. Again the old woman sat down without a word. Childe Charity scraped the pots for her supper, and slept on the sack.

In the morning the old woman was gone; but for six nights after, as sure as the supper was spread, there was she at the back door, and the little girl regularly asked her in.

Childe Charity's aunt said she would let her get enough of beggars. Her cousins made continual game of what they called her genteel visitor. Sometimes the old woman said: "Child, why don't you make this bed softer? and why are your blankets so thin?" but she never gave her a word of thanks, nor a civil good morning.

At last, on the ninth night from her first coming, when Childe Charity was getting used to scrape the pots and sleep on the sack, her accustomed knock came at the door, and there she stood with an ugly ashy-coloured dog, so stupid-looking and clumsy that no herd-boy would keep him.

"Good evening, my little girl," she said when Childe Charity opened the door. "I will not have your supper and bed to-night—I am going on a long journey to see a friend. But here is a dog of mine, whom nobody in all the west country will keep for me. He is a little cross, and not very handsome; but I leave him to your care till the shortest day in all the year. Then you and I will count for his keeping."

When the old woman had said the last word, she set off with such speed that Childe Charity lost sight of her in a minute. The ugly dog began to fawn upon her, but he snarled at everybody else. The servants said he was a disgrace to the house. The proud cousins wanted him drowned, and it was with great trouble that Childe Charity got leave to keep him in an old ruined cow-house.

Ugly and cross as the dog was, he fawned on her, and the old woman had left him to her care. So the little girl gave him part of all her meals, and when the hard frost came, took him privately to her own back garret, because the cow-house was damp and cold in the long nights. The dog lay quietly on some straw in a corner. Childe Charity slept soundly, but every morning the servants would say to her:—

"What great light and fine talking was that in your back garret?"

"There was no light, but the moon shining in through the shutterless window, and no talk that I heard," said Childe Charity.

And she thought they must have been dreaming. But night after night, when any of them awoke in the dark and silent hour that comes before the morning, they saw a light brighter and clearer than the Christmas fire, and heard voices like those of lords and ladies in the back garret.

Partly from fear, and partly from laziness, none of the servants would rise to see what might be there. At length, when the winter nights were at the longest, the little parlour-maid, who did least work and got most favour, because she gathered news for her mistress, crept out of bed when all the rest were sleeping, and set herself to watch at a crevice of the door.

She saw the dog lying quietly in the corner, Childe Charity sleeping soundly in her bed, and the moon shining through the shutterless window. But an hour before daybreak there came a glare of lights, and a sound of far-off bugles. The window opened, and in marched a troop of little men clothed in crimson and gold, and bearing every man a torch, till the room looked bright as day. They marched up with great reverence to the dog, where he lay on the straw, and the most richly clothed among them said:—

"Royal Prince, we have prepared the banquet hall. What will Your Highness please that we do next?"

"Ye have done well," said the dog. "Now, prepare the feast, and see that all things be in our first fashion: for the Princess and I mean to bring a stranger who never feasted in our halls before."

"Your Highness's commands shall be obeyed," said the little man, making another reverence; and he and his company passed out of the window.

By and by there was another glare of lights, and a sound like far-off flutes. The window opened, and there came in a company of little ladies clad in rose-coloured velvet, and carrying each a crystal lamp. They also walked with great reverence up to the dog, and the gayest among them said:—

"Royal Prince, we have prepared the tapestry. What will Your Highness please that we do next?"

"Ye have done well," said the dog. "Now, prepare the robes, and let all things be in our first fashion: for the Princess and I will bring with us a stranger who never feasted in our halls before."

"Your Highness's commands shall be obeyed," said the little lady, making a low curtsy; and she and her company passed out through the window, which closed quietly behind them.

The dog stretched himself out upon the straw, the little girl turned in her sleep, and the moon shone in on the back garret.

The parlour-maid was so much amazed, and so eager to tell this great story to her mistress, that she could not close her eyes that night, and was up before cock-crow. But when she told it, her mistress called her a silly wench to have such foolish dreams, and scolded her so that the parlour-maid durst not mention what she had seen to the servants.

Nevertheless Childe Charity's aunt thought there might be something in it worth knowing; so next night, when all the house were asleep, she crept out of bed, and set herself to watch at the back garret door.

There she saw exactly what the maid told her—the little men with the torches, and the little ladies with the crystal lamps, come in making great reverence to the dog, and the same words pass, only he said to the one, "Now prepare the presents," and to the other, "Prepare the jewels."

And when they were gone the dog stretched himself on the straw, Childe Charity turned in her sleep, and the moon shone in on the back garret.

The mistress could not close her eyes any more than the maid from eagerness to tell the story. She woke up Childe Charity's rich uncle before cock-crow. But when he heard it, he laughed at her for a foolish woman, and advised her not to repeat the like before the neighbours, lest they should think she had lost her senses.

The mistress could say no more, and the day passed. But that night the master thought he would like to see what went on in the back garret: so when all the house were asleep, he slipped out of bed, and set himself to watch at the crevice in the door.

The same thing happened again that the maid and the mistress saw: the little men in crimson with their torches, and the little ladies in rose-coloured velvet with their lamps, came in at the window, and made an humble reverence to the ugly dog, the one saying, "Royal Prince, we have prepared the presents," and the other, "Royal Prince, we have prepared the jewels."

And the dog said to them all: "Ye have done well. To-morrow come and meet me and the Princess with horses and chariots, and let all things be in our first fashion: for we will bring a stranger from this house who has never travelled with us, nor feasted in our halls before."

The little men and the little ladies said: "Your Highness's commands shall be obeyed."

When they had gone out through the window the ugly dog stretched himself out on the straw, Childe Charity turned in her sleep, and the moon shone in on the back garret.

The master could not close his eyes any more than the maid or the mistress, for thinking of this strange sight. He remembered to have heard his grandfather say, that somewhere near his meadows there lay a path leading to the Fairies' country, and the haymakers used to see it shining through the grey Summer morning as the Fairy bands went home. Nobody had heard or seen the like for many years; but the master concluded that the doings in his back garret must be a Fairy business, and the ugly dog a person of great account. His chief wonder was, however, what visitor the Fairies intended to take from his house; and after thinking the matter over he was sure it must be one of his daughters—they were so handsome, and had such fine clothes.

Accordingly, Childe Charity's rich uncle made it his first business that morning to get ready a breakfast of roast mutton for the ugly dog, and carry it to him in the old cow-house. But not a morsel would the dog taste. On the contrary, he snarled at the master, and would have bitten him if he had not run away with his mutton.

"The Fairies have strange ways," said the master to himself. But he called his daughters privately, bidding them dress themselves in their best, for he could not say which of them might be called into great company before nightfall.

Childe Charity's proud cousins, hearing this, put on the richest of their silks and laces, and strutted like peacocks from kitchen to parlour all day, waiting for the call their father spoke of, while the little girl scoured and scrubbed in the dairy.

They were in very bad humour when night fell, and nobody had come. But just as the family were sitting down to supper the ugly dog began to bark, and the old woman's knock was heard at the back door. Childe Charity opened it, and was going to offer her bed and supper as usual, when the old woman said:—

"This is the shortest day in all the year, and I am going home to hold a feast after my travels. I see you have taken good care of my dog, and now if you will come with me to my house, he and I will do our best to entertain you. Here is our company."

As the old woman spoke there was a sound of far-off flutes and bugles, then a glare of lights; and a great company, clad so grandly that they shone with gold and jewels, came in open chariots, covered with gilding, and drawn by snow-white horses.

The first and finest of the chariots was empty. The old woman led Childe Charity to it by the hand, and the ugly dog jumped in before her. The proud cousins, in all their finery, had by this time come to the door, but nobody wanted them. And no sooner was the old woman and her dog within the chariot than a marvellous change passed over them, for the ugly old woman turned at once to a beautiful young Princess, with long yellow curls and a robe of green and gold, while the ugly dog at her side started up a fair young Prince, with nut-brown hair, and a robe of purple and silver.

"We are," said they, as the chariots drove on, and the little girl sat astonished, "a Prince and Princess of Fairyland, and there was a wager between us whether or not there were any good people still to be found in these false and greedy times. One said 'Yes,' and the other said 'No'; and I have lost," said the Prince, "and must pay the feast and presents."

Some of the farmer's household, who were looking after them through the moonlight night, said the chariots had gone one way across the meadows, some said they had gone another, and till this day they cannot agree upon the direction.

But Childe Charity went with that noble company into a

country such as she had never seen—for Primroses covered all the ground, and the light was always like that of a Summer evening. They took her to a royal palace, where there was nothing but feasting and dancing for seven days. She had robes of pale green velvet to wear, and slept in a chamber inlaid with ivory.

When the feast was done, the Prince and Princess gave her such heaps of gold and jewels that she could not carry them, but they gave her a chariot to go home in, drawn by six white horses. And on the seventh night, which happened to be Christmas time, when the farmer's family had settled in their own minds that she would never come back, and were sitting down to supper, they heard the sound of her coachman's bugle, and saw her alight with all the jewels and gold at the very back door where she had brought in the ugly old woman.

The Fairy chariot drove away, and never came back to that farmhouse after. But Childe Charity scrubbed and scoured no more, for she grew a great lady, even in the eyes of her proud cousins.

The Shining Child and
the Wicked Mouche

(Adapted)

HOW THE RICH COUSINS CAME

O nce upon a time a noble but poor Count lived in the lovely
land of Alsace. He dwelt in a charming little house on a hill.
All around the house the graceful trees stretched out their leafy
branches like arms, as if they were saying: "Welcome! Welcome
among us!" Not far from the house was a thick green wood filled
with birds and flowers and scented grasses. The good Count did
not live alone in this delightful spot; no indeed, his wife and his
two children, Fanchon and Frederic, lived with him, happy and
contented.

Now, one Summer the news arrived that a wealthy and distinguished nobleman, cousin of the Count, was coming the next
day, with his family, to call upon his poor relatives.

The following morning the Countess got up very early, and
baked a cake into which she put more almonds and raisins than
she ever put into her Easter cakes, so that its delicious fragrance
filled the house. The Count dusted and brushed his old green
waistcoat; while Fanchon and Frederic, dressed in their best
clothes, sat waiting for the guests to come.

"You must not run about in the wood, as you usually do," said
the Count to them, "but sit very still so that you will look clean
and neat when your cousins arrive."

So the poor children were forced to stay in the house. The
morning sun was peeping bright and smiling from behind a
cloud, and was darting his rays in at the window. Out in the
wood the breeze was blowing sweet and fresh, and the robins,
the thrushes, the goldfinches, and the nightingales, were all warbling their loveliest songs. Poor Fanchon sat still and listened,

171

sometimes smoothing the bow on her pink sash, and sometimes knitting a bit, and all the while longing to run away to the wood. As for Frederic, he was looking at a picture book, but he kept jumping up every minute to gaze out at the window; for the big house dog Pepin was barking and bounding before the window, as if to say: "Aren't you coming out? What in the world are you doing in that stuffy room?"

And so Fanchon and Frederic had to remain in the house; and this was all the more painful, because the company-cake, which was on the table, gave out the most delicious spicy odours, yet might not be cut until the cousins came. "Oh! that they would only come!—would only come!" the children cried, and almost wept with impatience.

At last the loud tramping of horses was heard, and the rumble of wheels, then a carriage approached, so brilliant and so covered with golden ornaments that the children were amazed, for they had never seen anything like it. The carriage stopped before the house, and a very tall, thin gentleman glided out with the help of a footman, and fell into the arms of the Count, to whose cheek he gently pressed his lips. Then the footman aided a stout, red-faced woman to alight, while two children, a boy and a girl, stepped languidly down after her.

When they were all safely in the house, Fanchon and Frederic came forward and curtsied politely, as their father had told them to do. Then each seized a hand of the tall gentleman, saying: "We are glad you are come, noble Cousin!" After which they permitted the red-faced lady to embrace them; then they went up to the children, but stood before them silent and amazed. Indeed, these rich children were wonderfully dressed! The boy wore a little jacket of scarlet cloth, embroidered with gold and ornamented with gold tassels. A bright little sword hung at his side. On his head was a curious red cap with a white feather, from under which peeped his yellow face and bleared eyes.

The little girl had on a white dress all ribbons, lace, and bows, and her hair was frizzled and curled into a knot, on top of which was a shining coronet. Fanchon plucked up courage, and was going to take the little girl's hand, but she snatched it away in such a hurry and looked so tearful and angry, that Fanchon was frightened and let her alone.

Frederic wished to have a closer look at the boy's sword, and put out his hand to touch it, when the youngster began to shout and cry: "My sword! My sword! he is going to take my sword!" and ran to his father and hid behind him.

After that Fanchon and Frederic stood back quietly, while their mother cut the cake, and the older people talked. The two rich children sat munching dry crackers, for their parents said that cake was not good for them. But Fanchon and Frederic each had a large slice, which their dear mother gave them.

After they had finished eating, the guests arose to say good-bye, and the glittering carriage was driven to the door. The footman took from it two large bandboxes. These, the rich children handed with condescending pride, to Fanchon and Frederic. And just as the guests were about to take their leave, the dog Pepin, Frederic's faithful friend and darling, came dancing and barking around them. The rich children screamed, and had to be lifted, kicking with fright, into the carriage, which immediately drove away.

So ended the visit of these wealthy, distinguished, and noble cousins.

THE NEW PLAYTHINGS

After the carriage containing the wealthy cousins had rolled down the hill, the Count threw off his green waistcoat, and put on his loose jacket, and ran his fingers through his hair. The children, too, quickly got out of their best clothes, and felt light and happy.

"To the wood! To the wood!" shouted Frederic, jumping as high as he could for joy.

"But don't you wish to see what is in these handsome bandboxes your cousins gave you?" asked his mother.

And Fanchon, who had been gazing at the bandboxes with longing eyes, cried out: "Can't we open them first, and go to the wood afterward?"

But Frederic was hard to convince. "Surely that stupid boy could not have brought anything worth while," said he scornfully, "nor his ribbony sister! He talked so boldly about bears and lions, but when my dear Pepin barked, he forgot his sword and hid under the table! A brave sportsman he!"

"Oh, dear, good brother!" cried Fanchon, "just let us take one peep at what is in the boxes!"

So Frederic, who always did what he could to please his sister, gave up the idea of being off to the wood at once, and sat down patiently beside the table where the bandboxes were.

The mother opened them—and then—oh, my dear readers, if you could have seen what lay within! The loveliest toys were in those boxes! and candies, and sweet cakes, and nuts! The children clapped their hands again and again, crying: "Oh, how nice! Oh, how delicious!"

They took them all out of the boxes, and piled them on the table. None of the toys caused Frederic such satisfaction as did a little hunter who, when a string that stuck out from his jacket was pulled, put a gun to his shoulder, and fired at a target. Next to him in Frederic's affections, was a little fellow who bowed, and twanged on a harp, whenever Frederic turned a tiny handle. And, what pleased him nearly as much, was a shotgun of wood and a hunting pouch and belt.

Fanchon was equally delighted with a beautiful doll, a trunk filled with doll's dresses, tiny shoes, hats, and other lovely clothes, and a set of charming doll's furniture.

The two children forgot all about the wood, and enjoyed themselves with their playthings until quite late in the evening. They then went to bed and slept soundly.

WHAT HAPPENED TO THE PLAYTHINGS IN THE WOOD

The next morning, the children got their boxes and took out the playthings, and began to play. Then, just as on the day before, the sun shone brightly in at the window, the trees rustled in the breeze, and the birds sang their loveliest songs. At last Frederic cried out:—

"Why do we sit here in this stuffy room? I'll tell you what we'll do! Come, Fanchon, let us be off to the wood!"

Fanchon had just undressed her doll, and was going to put it to bed. "Why can't we stay here?" she begged, "and play a little longer, Frederic?"

"I'll tell you what we'll do," he replied. "We'll take our toys out to the wood. I'll put on my pouch and belt, and carry my gun. I'll be a real sportsman! The hunter and the harper may come, too. And you may take your doll. Come along! Let's be off!"

Fanchon hastened to dress her doll, then they both ran out of the house, and off to the wood. There they sat down on a nice grassy spot. And after they had played a while, Fanchon said:—

"Do you know, Frederic, that harper of yours does not play very well. Just listen how funny his harp sounds out here in the wood—with that eternal *ting! ting! ping! ping!*"

Frederic turned the handle more violently. "You're right, Fanchon," said he. "What the little fellow plays sounds quite horrible. He must make a better job of it!"

And with that he unscrewed the handle with such force, that—*crack! crack!*—the box on which the harper stood flew into a thousand splinters, and the arms of the little fellow were broken and hung useless at his sides.

"Oh! Oh!" cried Frederic.

"Ah, the poor little harper!" sighed Fanchon.

"Well, he was a stupid creature!" said Frederic. "He played very poor music, and bowed, and made faces like our yellow-faced cousin who gave him to us." And as Frederic spoke, he threw the harper into a thicket.

"What I like, is my hunter," he continued. "He hits the bull's eye every time he flies." And with that Frederic jerked the string so violently that—*twang! twang!*—the target was broken and the little man's arms hung limp and motionless.

"Ah! Ah!" cried Frederic. "You could shoot at your target in-doors, but out here, you can't shoot at all!" And so saying, Frederic, with all his might, shied the hunter after the harper into the thicket.

"Come, let us run about a bit," said he to Fanchon.

"Ah, yes! let us," said she. "This lovely doll of mine shall run with us. It will be great fun!"

So Fanchon and Frederic took each an arm of the doll, and off they ran through the bushes, on and on, until they came to a small lake. There they stopped, and Frederic said:—

"Suppose we wait a minute. I have a gun now, and perhaps I may hit a duck among the rushes."

At that moment, Fanchon screamed out: "Oh! just look at my doll! What's the matter with her?"

Indeed, the poor thing was in a miserable condition. Neither Fanchon nor Frederic had been paying any attention to her, and the bushes had torn all the clothes off her back; both her legs were broken; while her pretty waxen face was covered with so many scratches that it was hideous to look at.

"Oh! my beautiful, beautiful child!" sobbed Fanchon.

"There, you see what a stupid creature that doll of yours is!" cried Frederic. "She can't even take a little run, but she must tear and spoil her clothes! Give her to me!"

And before Fanchon could say a word, or cry: "Oh! Oh!" Frederic snatched the doll, and flung her into the lake.

"Never mind, Fanchon!" said he consolingly. "Never mind, if I can shoot a duck, you shall have the most beautiful wing-feathers."

Just then a noise was heard among the rushes, and Frederic instantly took aim with his wooden gun. But he dropped it quickly from his shoulder, saying:—

"Am I not an idiot! How can a fellow shoot a duck without powder and shot? What's the use of this stupid wooden thing, anyway?" With that he flung the gun and his pouch and belt into the lake.

But poor Fanchon was weeping at the loss of her doll, and Frederic was annoyed at the way things had turned out, so they both crept back sadly to the house. And when their mother asked them what had become of the playthings, Frederic truthfully related how they had been deceived by the harper, the hunter, the doll, and all.

"Ah! you foolish children!" cried their mother half in anger, "you do not deserve to have nice toys!"

But the Count, who had been listening to Frederic's tale, said:

"Let the children alone. I am really glad that they are fairly rid of those playthings. There was something queer about them."

But neither the children nor their mother understood what the Count meant.

THE STRANGER CHILD

Soon after these events very early one morning Fanchon and Frederic ran off to the wood. They were feeling sad, for their mother had told them that they must return home soon to study, so as to be ready for the tutor that their rich cousin had promised to send them. For the tutor was expected shortly.

"Let us run and jump as much as we can now," said Frederic, when they reached the wood, "for in a little while we shall not be allowed to stay out here at all!"

So they began to play hide-and-seek, but everything went wrong. The wind carried Frederic's hat into the bushes. He stumbled and fell on his nose as he was running. Fanchon found herself hanging by her clothes on a thorn-tree, and she banged her foot against a sharp stone so that she shrieked with pain. In fact the children could not understand what was the matter with them on this particular day; and they gave up their game, and slunk dejectedly through the wood. Frederic threw himself down under a shady tree, and Fanchon followed his example. And there the two children lay gloomy and wretched, gazing on the ground.

"Ah!" said Fanchon, "if we only had our playthings!"

"Nonsense!" said Frederic, "what should we do with them? I'll tell you what it is, Fanchon, Mother is right, I suspect. The toys were good enough, but we didn't know how to play with them. If we were as learned as our rich cousins, we should be so wise that all our toys would now be whole; and we should know how to play with them rightly."

And at that Fanchon began to sob and cry bitterly, and Frederic joined her; and they both howled and lamented until the wood rang again and again: "Oh! poor, unfortunate children that we are! Oh! that we were as wise as our cousins!"

But suddenly they both stopped crying, and asked each other in amazement:—

"Do you hear anything, Fanchon?"

"Do you hear anything, Frederic?"

For out of the deepest shade of the dark thicket in front of the children, a wonderful brightness began to shine, playing like moonlight over the leaves that trembled as if in joy. Then through the whispering trees came a sweet musical note, like the sound of a harp. The children lay motionless with awe. All their sorrow passed away from them, and tender, happy tears rose into their eyes.

As the radiance streamed brighter and brighter through the bushes, and the marvellous music grew louder and louder, the children's hearts beat high. They gazed eagerly at the brightness. Then they saw, smiling at them from the thicket, the most beautiful face of a child, with the sun beaming on it in splendour.

"Oh! come to us!—Come to us!—darling Shining Child!" cried Fanchon and Frederic, stretching out their arms; and their hearts were filled with an indescribable longing.

"I am coming! I am coming!" a sweet voice cried from the bushes.

And then, as if borne on the wings of the breeze, the Stranger Child seemed to float hovering toward Fanchon and Frederic.

HOW THE SHINING CHILD PLAYED
WITH FANCHON AND FREDERIC

"What is the matter, dear children?" asked the Stranger Child. "I heard you crying and lamenting, and I was very sorry for you! What do you want?"

"Ah!" said Frederic, "we did not know what we wanted; but now I see that we wanted *you*—just you yourself!"

"That's it!" chimed in Fanchon. "Now that you are with us, we are happy again! Why were you so long in coming?"

In fact both children felt as if they had known and played with the Stranger Child all their lives, and that their unhappiness had been because their beloved playmate was not with them.

"You see," Frederic added, "we have no toys left, for I, like a stupid dolt, broke all our fine things, and shied them into the thicket."

At this the Stranger Child laughed merrily, and cried: "Why, Fanchon and Frederic, you are lying this minute among the loveliest playthings that ever were seen!"

"Where?—Where are they?" Fanchon and Frederic both cried.

"Look around you," said the Stranger Child.

Then Fanchon and Frederic saw how out of the thick grass and moss all sorts of glorious flowers were peeping, with bright eyes gleaming. And between them many coloured stones and crystal shells sparkled and shone. While little golden insects danced up and down humming gentle songs.

"Now we will build a palace!" said the Stranger Child. "Help me to get the stones together." And it stooped down and began to pick up stones of many pretty colours.

Fanchon and Frederic helped, and the Stranger Child placed the beautiful stones one upon another, and soon there rose tall pillars shining in the sun, while an airy golden roof stretched itself from pillar to pillar. Then the Stranger Child kissed the flowers that were peeping from the grass, and whispered to them lovingly, and they shot up higher and higher, and, twining together, formed sweet-scented arbours and covered walks in which the children danced about, full of delight and gladness.

The Stranger Child clapped its hands, and immediately the golden roof, that was made of insects' golden wings, fell to pieces with a hum, and the pillars melted away into a splashing silver stream, on whose banks flowers grew and peeped into the water.

Then the Stranger Child plucked little blades of grass and gathered twigs from trees, strewing them on the ground before Fanchon and Frederic. The blades of grass turned into the prettiest little live dolls ever seen, and the twigs became gay little huntsmen.

The dolls danced around Fanchon, and let her take them in her lap, and they whispered in such delicate little voices: "Be kind to us! Love us, dear Fanchon."

The huntsmen shouted: "Halloa! Halloa! the hunt's up!" and blew their horns, and bustled about. Then tiny hares came darting out of the bushes, with tiny dogs after them, and the huntsmen pursued them with shouts. This was delightful!

Then suddenly these wonders disappeared. And Fanchon and Frederic cried out: "What has become of the dolls? Where are the huntsmen?"

The Stranger Child answered: "Oh, they are always here waiting for you! They are close beside you, so you may have them at any minute. But just now would you not rather go with me through the wood?"

"Oh, yes! yes!" cried Fanchon and Frederic.

The Stranger Child took hold of their hands, crying: "Come! Come!"

And with that off they went! The children felt themselves floating along lightly and easily, through the trees; while all the birds flew fluttering beside them, singing and warbling their sweetest songs. Then suddenly up they soared into the air. Higher and higher they mounted like birds, skimming above the tops of the trees. Frederic shouted with delight, but Fanchon was frightened.

"Oh, my breath is going! I shall tumble!" she cried.

And just at that moment the Stranger Child let them down gently to the ground, and said: "Now I shall sound my Forest-Song. Then good-bye for to-day."

And the Stranger Child took out a little horn of wreathed gold, and began to sound it so beautifully that the whole wood reëchoed wondrously with its lovely music; while a host of nightingales came flocking to the branches above the children's heads, and sang their most melodious songs.

But all at once the music grew fainter and fainter, and only a soft whispering seemed to come from the thicket into which the Stranger Child had vanished.

"To-morrow! To-morrow! I will come again!" the children heard breathed gently as if from a distance. Then they sighed with joy, for, though they could not understand it, never had they known such happiness in all their lives.

"Oh! I wish it was to-morrow, now!" they both cried, as they hastened home to their parents.

HOW THE FOREST TALKED
TO FANCHON AND FREDERIC

"I should fancy that the children had dreamed all this," said the Count to his wife, when Fanchon and Frederic, who could think of nothing else but the Stranger Child, and the wonderful events, and the exquisite music, had told all that had happened. "I should fancy that they had dreamed all this, if they had not both seen the same things! I cannot get to the bottom of it all!"

"Don't bother your head about it, my dear," answered his wife. "I think this Stranger Child was nobody but the school-master's son from the village. We must take care that he is not allowed to put any more such nonsense into the children's heads."

But the Count could not agree with her, for he called the children to him again, to tell how the Stranger Child was dressed and looked. Fanchon and Frederic both agreed that its face was fair as lilies, that it had cheeks like roses, cherry lips, bright blue eyes, and locks of gold; and that it was more beautiful than words could tell.

But what they said about its dress sounded absurd. For Fanchon said that its dress was wondrous beautiful, shining and gleaming, as if made of the petals of flowers; while Frederic insisted that its garments were of sparkling golden-green, like spring-leaves in the sunshine.

And Frederic thought that the Stranger Child was a boy; while Fanchon was sure that it was a girl. And these contradictions confused their parents; and the Count shook his head wonderingly.

The next day, Fanchon and Frederic hastened to the wood, and found the Stranger Child waiting for them. If their play had been glorious the day before, it was ten times more glorious to-day; for the Stranger Child did such marvellous things that Fanchon and Frederic shouted for joy.

While they played, the Stranger Child talked sweetly to the trees, flowers, and birds, and to the brook that ran through the wood; and they all answered so clearly that Fanchon and Frederic understood everything they said.

"Dear children!" cried the Alder-thicket, "why were you not

here early, when my friend the Morning Breeze came rustling over the blue hills, and brought us thousands of greetings and kisses from the Golden Queen of the Dawn, and plenty of wing-waftings full of sweet perfumes!"

"Oh, silence!" the flowers broke in. "Do not mention that robber, the Morning Breeze! Does he not steal our perfumes! Never mind the Alders, children, let them lisp and whisper. Listen to us! We love you so! We dress ourselves in the loveliest colours just for you!"

"And do we not love *you*, you beautiful flowers!" said the Stranger Child tenderly.

But Fanchon knelt down on the grass, and stretched out her arms, as if she would take all the bright flowers to her heart, and cried: "Ah! I love you! I love you every one!"

Then came a sighing out of the tall dark firtrees, and they said: "We shade the flowers from the hot sun, and shelter human children when the storm comes rushing through the woods, but who loves us in return?"

"Groan and sigh," cried Frederic, "and murmur as much as you like, you green giants that you are! It is then that the real woodsman's heart rejoices in you! I love all, the green bushes, the flowers, and you trees!"

"You are quite right!" splashed the brook as it sparkled over its stones. "Come sit down among this moss, dear children, and listen to me. I come from afar; out of a deep, cool, dark rock I gush. Look into my waves, and I will show you the loveliest pictures in my clear mirror, the blue of the sky, the fleecy clouds, bushes, trees, and blossoms; and your very selves, dear children, I draw tenderly into my transparent bosom!"

"Fanchon and Frederic," said the Stranger Child, looking around with wondrous blissfulness. "Only listen how they all love us! But the redness of evening is rising behind the hills, and the nightingale is calling me home!"

"Oh, but first let us fly a little, as we did yesterday!" begged Frederic.

"Yes," said Fanchon, "but not quite so high. It makes my head giddy."

Then the Stranger Child took them each by the hand again, and they went soaring up into the golden purple of the evening sky, while the birds crowded and sang around them.

Among the shining clouds, Frederic saw, as if in wavering flame, beautiful castles all of rubies and other precious stones.

"Look! Look! Fanchon!" he cried, full of rapture. "Look at those splendid palaces! Let us fly along as fast as we can, and we shall soon get to them."

Fanchon, too, saw the castles, and forgot her fear, and kept looking upward.

"Those are my beloved castles-in-the-air," the Stranger Child said. "But we must go no farther to-day!"

Fanchon and Frederic seemed to be in a dream, and could not make out how they suddenly came to find themselves with their father and mother.

THE PALACE OF THE FAIRY QUEEN

It was the next day. In the most beautiful part of the wood beside the brook, between whispering bushes, the Stranger Child had set up a glorious tent made of tall slender lilies, glowing roses, and tulips of every hue. And beneath this tent, Fanchon and Frederic were seated with the Stranger Child, listening to the forest brook as it whirled, and rippled, and sang its wonderful stories.

"Tell us," said Fanchon, "darling Shining Child, where your home is, and all about your father and mother."

The Stranger Child looked sorrowfully at the sky. "Ah, my dear," it said with a sigh, "is it not enough that I come to you each day? Why must you then ask about my home? Though you were to travel day after day, forever and ever, even to beyond the utmost range of the purple hills, you could not reach it!"

"Ah me!" sighed Fanchon. "Then you must live hundreds and hundreds of miles away from us! Is it only on a visit that you are here?"

"Fanchon, beloved," said the Stranger Child, "whenever you

long for me with all your heart, I am with you immediately, bringing you all those plays and wonders. Is that not as good as being in my home?"

"Not at all," said Frederic, "for I believe that you live in a most glorious palace. I do not care how hard the road is to your home, I mean to set out for this minute for it."

"And so you shall!" said the Stranger Child smiling; "for when you see all this so clearly before you, and make up your mind to be there, it is as good as done! The land where I live, in truth, is so beautiful and glorious that I can give you no description of it. It is my mother who reigns over that land,—all glory and loveliness—as Queen."

"Ah! you are a Prince!" cried Frederic.

"Ah! you are a Princess!' cried Fanchon.

"I certainly am," said the Stranger Child. "My mother's palace is far more beautiful than those glittering castles you saw in the evening clouds. For the gleaming pillars of her palace are of the purest crystal, and they soar slender and tall into the blue of heaven. Upon them rests a great, wide blue canopy. Beneath the canopy sail the shining white clouds, hither and thither on golden wings. And the red of the evening and the morning rises and falls, and the sparkling stars dance in a singing circle around her palace.

"You have heard of the Fairies who can bring about great wonders. My mother is Queen of the Fairies. Very often she holds a feast for little children. It is then that the Elves, belonging to my mother's Kingdom, fly through the air weaving shining rainbows from one end of her palace to the other. Under these rainbows they build my mother's diamond throne,—that in appearance and perfume is like lilies, roses, and carnations.

"My mother takes her place upon the throne, and the Elves sing, and play on golden harps. As soon as their music begins, everything in the palace and in the woods and gardens, moves and sings. And all around there are thousands of beautiful little children in charming dresses, shouting with delight.

"The children chase each other among the golden trees, and throw blossoms at each other. They climb the trees where the wind swings and rocks them. They gather gold-glittering fruit,

and they play with tame deer and other gentle wild creatures,
that come bounding up to them and lick their hands. Then the
children run up and down the rainbows; or they ride on the
backs of great Purple Birds that fly up among the gleaming
clouds.

"How delightful that must be!" cried Fanchon and Frederic,
with rapture. "Oh! take us with you to your home, beautiful
Shining Child! We want to stay there always!'

"That may not be," said the Stranger Child.

And Fanchon and Frederic cast down their eyes sadly to the
ground.

THE WICKED MOUCHE

"Ah," said the Stranger Child, "you might not be so happy at
my mother's Court. Indeed, it would be a great misfortune for
you to try to go to her Kingdom. There are many children who
cannot bear the singing of the Purple Birds, and, if they hear
their songs, they die. Then too, destruction might overtake you
before you could reach my mother's Court. Even I am not safe
on my way thither.

'There was a time when I was safe anywhere. But now a bitter enemy of my mother, whom she banished from her
Kingdom, goes raging about the world; and I cannot be safe
from being watched, pursued, and molested. Powerless as this
bitter enemy is when I am at home, nothing can protect me
from him, when I am flying abroad."

"What sort of a hateful creature is it," asked Fanchon, "that
can do you so much harm?"

"I have told you," said the Stranger Child, "that my mother is
the Fairy Queen. Among her many Elves are some who hover in
the sky, or dwell in the waters, and others who serve at the Fairy
Court. Once, a long while ago, there came among those that
served at Court, a stranger who called himself Papillon. He said
that he was learned in all the sciences of the world, and could
accomplish great things among us. My mother made him prime
minister.

"Papillon soon showed his natural spite and wickedness. He pretended to the Queen that he loved children and could make them very happy. But instead of doing so, he hung himself like a weight of lead on the tails of the Purple Birds, so that they could not fly aloft. And when the children climbed the rose-trees, he dragged them down by the legs. Then he knocked their noses on the ground, and made them bleed. When the children sang, he crammed all sorts of nasty stuff down their throats; for sweet and happy singing he could not abide. And worst of all, he had a way of smearing the sparkling precious stones of the palace, and the lilies and roses, and even the shining rainbows, with a horrible black juice, so that everything beautiful became sorrowful or dead.

"And when he had done all this, he gave a loud hissing laugh, and said that everything was now as he wished it to be. Then, shouting that he was greater than my mother, he went flying up into the air, in the shape of an enormous fly with flashing eyes, and a long snout. After which he went humming and buzzing around my mother's throne, in a most abominable fashion.

"When the Queen my mother and her Elves saw this, they knew that he had come among them under a false name, and that he was none other than Mouche, the gloomy King of the Gnomes. The entire Fairy Court thereupon rushed against him beating him with their wings, while the Purple Birds seized him with their glittering beaks and gripped him so tightly that he screamed with agony and rage. After which the birds shook him violently, and threw him down to the earth. He fell straight onto the back of his old Aunt, who was a great blue toad. And she carried him off to her hole.

"But five hundred of the children in the Fairy Court armed themselves with fly-flappers, to defend themselves against the Mouche if he should ever venture to return. Now after he was gone, all the black juice disappeared, and everything became as shining and glorious as before.

"So you see, dear Children," continued the Stranger Child, "what kind of a creature I have to fear. This horrible Mouche follows me about, and, if I did not hide myself quickly, he would injure me. And I assure you that if I were to take you with me to my home, Mouche would lie in wait for us, and kill us."

Fanchon wept bitterly at the danger to which the Stranger Child was exposed. But Frederic said: "If that horrible Mouche is nothing but a great fly, I'll soon hit him with father's big fly-flapper! And if once I give him a good crack on his nose, Aunty Blue Toad will have a job carrying him to her hole again!"

HOW TUTOR INK ARRIVED
TO TEACH THE CHILDREN

Fanchon and Frederic ran home as fast as they could, shouting as they went:—

"Oh! the Shining Child is a beautiful Princess!"

"Oh! the Shining Child is a beautiful Prince!"

They wanted, in their delight, to tell this to their parents, but their father came to meet them with a most extraordinary man walking by his side. This stranger kept muttering to himself:—

"What a nice pair of stupids these are! Ah! Ah!"

The Count took him by the hand, and said to the children: "This gentleman is the tutor whom your kind cousin has sent to teach you. So now shake hands with him, and bid him welcome."

But the children looked sidewise at him, and could move neither hand nor foot. This was because they had never seen such an extraordinary being. He was no taller than Frederic. His body was round and bloated, and his little weazen legs could hardly support its weight. His head was queer and square, and his face too ugly for anything, for not only was his nose long and pointed, but his little bulging eyes glittered, and his wide mouth was opened in a ferocious way. He was clad in black from top to toe, and his name was Tutor Ink.

Now, as the children stood staring like stone images, their mother cried out angrily: "You rude children, what are you thinking of? Come! come! give the tutor your hands."

The children, taking heart, did as their mother bade them. But as soon as Tutor Ink took hold of their hands, they jumped back, screaming: "Oh! Oh! It hurts!"

The tutor laughed aloud, and showed a needle, which he had hidden in his hand to prick the children with. Fanchon was weeping; but Frederic growled. "Just try that again, little Big-Body, if you dare!"

"Why did you do that, Tutor Ink?" asked the Count, some-what annoyed.

"Well, it's just my way!" answered Tutor Ink; "I can't alter it!" and with that he stuck his hands to his sides, and went on laugh-ing until his voice sounded like the noise of a broken rattle.

Alas! after that there was no more running about in the wood! Instead the children, day after day, had to sit in the house, repeating after Tutor Ink strange gibberish, not one word of which they could understand.

With what longing eyes they looked at the wood! Often they thought they heard, amidst the happy songs of the birds and the rustling of the trees, the voice of the Stranger Child, calling, and calling: "Fanchon! Frederic! Are you not coming to play with me? Oh, come! I have made you a palace all of flowers! We will play there, and I will give you all sorts of beautiful stones! And then we'll fly through the air, and build cloud-castles! Come! Oh, come!"

At this the children's thoughts were so drawn to the wood, that they neither heard nor saw their tutor any longer; although he thumped on the table with both his fists, and hummed, and growled, and snarled.

At last one day the Count perceived how pale the children were getting, and bade Tutor Ink take them for a walk. The Tutor did not like the idea at all. And the children did not like it either, saying:—

"What business has Tutor Ink in our darling wood?"

WHAT HAPPENED WHEN TUTOR INK
TOOK THE CHILDREN TO THE WOOD

"Well, Tutor Ink, is it not delightful here in our wood?" asked Frederic.

Tutor Ink made a face, and muttered: "Stupid nonsense! All one does is to tear his stockings! One can't hear a word because of the abominable screeching of the birds!"

"But surely you love the flowers!" Fanchon chimed in.

At this Tutor Ink's face became a deep cherry-colour, and he beat his hands about him, crying: "Stupid nonsense! Ridiculous nonsense! There are no decent flowers in this wood!"

"But don't you see those dear little Lilies-of-the-valley peeping up at you with such bright loving eyes?" asked Fanchon.

"What! What!" the Tutor screamed. "Flowers!—eyes?—Ha! Ha!—Nice eyes!—Useless things!" And with that he stooped, and plucking up a handful of the lilies, roots and all, threw them into the thicket.

Fanchon could not help shedding bitter tears, and Frederic gnashed his teeth in anger. Just then a little Robin alighted on a branch near the Tutor's head, and began to sing sweetly. The Tutor, picking up a stone, threw it, and the bird fell dying to the ground.

Frederic could restrain himself no longer. "You horrible Tutor Ink!" he cried, "what did the little bird do to you, that you should strike it dead?" And looking toward the thicket, he called sadly: "Oh! where are you, beautiful Shining Child? Oh, come! Only come! Let us fly far, far away! I cannot stay beside this horrible creature any longer."

And Fanchon, stretching out her hands, sobbed and wept bitterly. "Oh, you darling Shining Child," she cried. "Come to us! Come to us! Save us! Save us! Tutor Ink is killing us, as he is killing the flowers and birds!"

"What do you mean by the Shining Child?" snarled Tutor Ink.

But at that instant there was a loud whispering, and a rustling, in the thicket, and a sound as of muffled drums tolling in the distance. Then the children saw, in a shining cloud that floated above them, the beautiful face of the Stranger Child, and tears like glittering pearls were rolling down its rosy cheeks.

"Ah! darling playmates!" it cried. "I cannot come to you any more! Farewell! Farewell! The Gnome Mouche has you in his power! Oh! you poor children, good-bye! good-bye!"

And then the Stranger Child soared up far into the clouds. And the most marvellous thing happened! Behind the children there began a most horrid, fearsome buzzing and humming, snarling and growling, and, lo! Tutor Ink had changed into an enormous frightful-looking fly. And he began to fly upward heavily, following the Stranger Child.

Fanchon and Frederic, overpowered with terror, ran out of the wood, and did not dare to look up at the sky until they had got some distance away. And, then, when they did so, all that they could see, was a shining speck in the clouds, glittering like a star, and coming nearer and downward.

The star grew bigger and bigger, and the children could hear, as if it were, the call of a trumpet; and presently they saw that the star was really a splendid bird with shining purple plumage. It came dropping down to the wood, clapping its mighty wings, and singing loud and clear.

"Hurrah! Hurrah!" shouted Frederic. "That is a Purple Bird from the Fairy Court! He will bite Tutor Ink to death! The Shining Child is saved!—and so are we! Come, Fanchon, let us get home as fast as we can, and tell our father about it."

WHAT THE COUNT DID TO TUTOR INK

The children burst into the house where their parents were sitting.

"Hurrah! Hurrah!" Frederic shouted. "The Purple Bird has bitten Tutor Ink to death!"

"Oh, Father dear, Mother dear!" cried Fanchon. "Tutor Ink is not Tutor Ink at all! He is really the wicked Mouche, King of the Gnomes; a monstrous fly, but a fly with clothes and shoes and stockings on!"

"Who on earth has been putting such nonsense into your heads?" asked the Countess.

And the parents gazed at the children in utter amazement, while they went on to tell about the Stranger Child whose mother was a great Fairy Queen, and about the Gnome King, Mouche, and the Purple Bird.

The Count grew very grave and thoughtful. "Frederic," said he, "you are really a sensible boy, and I must admit that Tutor Ink has always seemed to me a strange mysterious creature. Your mother and I are by no means satisfied with him, particularly your mother. He has such a terrible sweet-tooth, that there's no way of keeping him from the sugar and jams. And, then, he hums and buzzes in such a distressing manner. But in spite of all this, my dear boy, just think calmly for a minute. Even if there are such things as Gnomes in the world, do you really mean to say that your Tutor has become a fly?"

Frederic looked his father steadily in the face with his clear blue eyes, then said:—

"I should not have believed it myself, if the Stranger Child had not said so, and if I had not seen with my own eyes that he is only a horrible fly, and pretends to be Tutor Ink. And then," continued Frederic, while his father shook his head in wonder, "see what Mother says about him. Is he not ravenous for sweet things? Is that not just like a fly? And then his hummings and buzzings."

"Silence," cried the Count. "Whatever Tutor Ink is, one thing is certain, the Purple Bird has not bitten him to death! for there he comes out of the wood!"

At this the children uttered loud screams, and rushed behind the door. In truth, Tutor Ink was approaching, but he was wild-looking and bewildered. He was buzzing and humming, and springing high in the air, first to one side, then to the other, and banging his head against the trees. He tumbled into the house, and dashed at the milk-jug, and popped his head into it so that the milk ran over the sides. Then he gulped and gulped, making a horrid noise of swallowing.

"What ails you, Tutor Ink?" cried the Countess. "What are you about?"

"Are you out of your senses?" asked the Count. "Is the foul fiend after you?"

But without making any answer, Tutor Ink, taking his mouth from the milk-jug, threw himself down on the dish of butter, and began to lick it with his pointed tongue. Then, with a loud buzzing, he sprang off the table and began to stagger hither and thither about the room, as though he was drunk.

"This is pretty behaviour!" cried the Count, as he tried to seize Tutor Ink by the coat tails; but Tutor Ink managed to elude him deftly.

Just then Frederic came running up with his father's big fly-flapper in his hand, and gave it to the Count, crying:—

""Here you are, Father! Knock the terrible Mouche to death!"

The Count took the fly-flapper; and then they all set to work to drive away Tutor Ink. Fanchon and Frederic and their mother took table napkins, and made sweeps with them in the air, driving the Tutor backward and forward, here and there, while the Count kept striking at him with the fly-flapper.

Wilder and wilder grew the chase. *"Hum! Hum!"* and *"Sum! Sum!"* went the Tutor, storming hither and thither. *"Flip! Flap!"* and *"Clip! Clap!"* went the table napkins and fly-flapper.

At last the Count managed to hit the Tutor's coat tails. Then just as the Count was going to strike a second time, up bounced the Tutor into the air, and, with renewed strength, stormed, humming and buzzing, out of the door, and away among the trees.

"Well done!" exclaimed the Count. "We are rid of that abominable Tutor Ink! Never shall he cross my threshold again!"

HOW THE NAUGHTY PLAYTHINGS BECAME ALIVE

Fanchon and Frederic now breathed freely once more. A great weight was taken off their hearts. They rejoiced that now, since the wicked Mouche was gone, the Stranger Child might come back. They hurried to the wood. Everything was silent and deserted. Not a merry note of a single bird was there. Instead of the joyous singing of the brook, and the gladsome rustling of the leaves, they seemed to hear sighs and moans that passed through the air. Just then, close behind them, snarling voices cried out:—

"Stupid creatures! Senseless creatures! You despised us! You did not know how to treat us! We are come back to punish you!"

Fanchon and Frederic looked around, and saw the little hunter and the harper rise out of the thicket. The harper twanged his tiny harp, while the hunter took aim at Frederic; and both cried out:—

"Wait, you boy and girl! We are obedient servants of Tutor Ink! He will be here in a moment, and then we'll pay you well for despising us!"

Terrified, the children turned to run away, when the doll rose up out of the thicket, and squeaked out:—

"Stupid creatures! Senseless creatures! I am an obedient servant of Tutor Ink! He will be here in a moment, and then I'll pay you well for despising me!" And with that the naughty creature sent great splashes of muddy water flying at Fanchon and Frederic, so that they were quite wet.

Then the children fell on their knees sobbing: "Oh, how unfortunate we are! Will no one take pity on us!"

Scarcely had they said thus, when the playthings disappeared. The rushing of the brook turned to the sweetest music. All the wood streamed with a wonderful sparkling light. And, lo! the Stranger Child came forth from the thicket, surrounded by such brilliant rays that Fanchon and Frederic had to shut their eyes for a minute.

Then they felt themselves touched gently, and the Stranger Child's sweet voice said:—

"Oh, do not mourn for me, dear playmates! Though you will not see me again, still I shall be near you. Neither the wicked Mouche nor any other Gnome shall have power to harm you. Only go on loving me faithfully."

"That we shall! that we shall! dear Shining Child!" the children cried. "We love you with all our hearts!"

And at last when they could open their eyes, the Stranger Child had vanished; and all their grief and fear were gone, too. Delight beamed in their eyes and shone in their cheeks.

And what the Stranger Child had said, came to pass. Nothing ever harmed Fanchon and Frederic. They grew up handsome, clever, and sweet-tempered; and all that they undertook prospered. And as the years went on, they still, in their dreams, played with the Stranger Child, who never ceased to bring them the loveliest things from its Fairy Home.